F.W. E.A.P. DOWMA

LEFT-HAND GUN

Grasping landowner Morgan Fetterman hires a professional gunman to get rid of Jemima Penrose from her ranch in the mountains of Arizona. However, his mistake is to choose Luke Horn for the job, because he dislikes what he hears about Fetterman. Then Horn, despite a disabling wound in his right arm, assists in getting rustlers brought to justice. But amid the plotting and gunplay, can Horn, Jemima and old guy Fed Sauermann bring Fetterman's plans tumbling down?

WALT MASTERSON

LEFT-HAND GUN

Complete and Unabridged

LINFORD
Leicester

First published in Great Britain in 2009 by
Robert Hale Limited
London

First Linford Edition
published 2010
by arrangement with
Robert Hale Limited
London

British Library CIP Data

Masterson, Walt.
  Left-hand gun.- -(Linford western library)
  1. Western stories.
  2. Large type books.
  I. Title II. Series
  823.9′2–dc22

  ISBN 978–1–44480–091–3

Published by
F. A. Thorpe (Publishing)
Anstey, Leicestershire

Set by Words & Graphics Ltd.
Anstey, Leicestershire
Printed and bound in Great Britain by
T. J. International Ltd., Padstow, Cornwall

This book is printed on acid-free paper

For all the boys at El Vino
who knew how to shoot a line.

1

The sun seemed unusually hot that day, as though Allen Springs had somehow drawn all the available rays into its own main street. The loungers slouched in their chairs on the shady side of the rutted dust that served as a roadway, the two horses at the hitching rail stood three-legged and hip-shot, twitching their tails at the flies.

Even the piano player in the Maverick saloon had gone to sleep in the heat, and George the barman had polished every single one of his glasses into a gloss so high that it hurt to look at them. Hurt George, anyway. He remarked on it. Often.

A man could hear the trouble coming a mile away. It came on trotting hoofs with a faint silvery jingle of harness chains and it stopped in front of the Maverick. There was a creak of saddle leather as the rider stepped down, and the sound of water splashing in the trough as the horse drank. A moment of peace, then heels sounded on the sidewalk.

George raised his head and stared at the door. The batwings flipped as he did so. The man who came through them paused as he pulled off his gloves, though his eyes were anything but restful. They quartered the empty room carefully and came to rest on George.

'Howdy,' said George, easily. 'Stranger in town, just passing through?'

The man did not reply immediately. He folded his gloves, tucked them into his hip pocket and walked slowly across the room.

He was a tall man and rangy, except about the shoulders, where he was downright, honest-to-betsy big. He wore normal range clothes: a dark wool shirt coated in dust, jeans and square-toed black riding-boots, with big silver spurs which whispered musically as he walked.

Like most men in the Arizona

Territory, he wore a gun. A black-handled Colt, on a black leather cartridge belt. Both the gun and the belt looked as though they had seen much use. So did the second pistol, tucked behind the brass buckle of his belt, its butt pointing to the left.

The barkeep gave the mahogany bar a professional sweep with his towel, set up a glass and said: 'Whiskey?'

'Got a cold beer?'

'One cold beer, coming right up,' said George, and it did. It was cold, too. Cold enough to mist the outside of the glass. The stranger looked at it for a moment through dreamy eyes, then reached out with his left hand and ran his finger down the outside of the glass, leaving a clear trail and a bead of moisture on the bar.

After some moments he picked up the glass, raised it to his lips and sank half the contents in one long swallow.

George swore later he could see the dark tanned face swell up as the liquid went down. This man, he said, was pure-dee dried out. He needed the beer and he surely did appreciate it, yes, sir! A man of words, was George.

'Just passing through?' he ventured. The stranger shook his head, and sank the other half of the beer, then put the glass back on the bar.

'Again,' he said. He was looking over George's head as he spoke, and the barkeep knew he watching the door in the mirror over the shelves at the back. He wondered uneasily if it was ingrained habit or if the newcomer had brought trouble with him.

He refilled the beer glass and put a shot glass next to it, with an enquiring look. The stranger shook his head.

'Just the beer,' he said. 'And directions.'

'Where to?'

'There's a ranch round here called Flatbush. What's the quickest way to get there?'

Flatbush. George might have known.

'Go out of town down the Tucson road, takes you straight past Boot Hill.

4

Save yourself a journey, mister. Go dig yourself a hole and climb right in, save us the trouble of coming out to the Flat to get your body and pack it right back into town.'

'Huh?' For the first time the gunbarrel eyes focused straight on him, instead of the mirror.

'That girl's got more of a title to that ranch than any mortal soul, including Morgan Fetterman. And she can shoot the eye out of a blowfly at a hundred yards. Leave her be, my advice.'

The unreadable eyes studied him, then checked on the mirror again.

'Whose horses are them out there?'

George realized he had been wasting his time, and abandoned the struggle.

'Couple of Fetterman hands from the Tumble B, which makes 'em your friends,' he said. 'Sort them out yourself. They're in the back, playing poker.'

'Don't sound like you take to 'em much.'

'They run too many people out of the country for my liking. I'll tell you something else, too. If you're expecting to work with them, camp out doors, sleep alone and watch your back trail.' He stopped, suddenly aware that he had said too much.

There was a flicker of amusement in the tanned face, and the man touched his hat with the forefinger of his left hand.

'Obliged, friend,' he said, dropped coins on the bar and turned for the door. As he went the tiny tinkle of the chains on his spurs gave off a musical chink at each step. The barkeep found himself heaving a gusty sigh of relief as the batwing doors flapped and, outside, leather creaked as the man stepped into his saddle.

Hoofbeats receded down the road. A fly buzzed at the drops of drying beer on the bar, and he flicked it into ruin with the end of his glass cloth.

★ ★ ★

It was twenty minutes before the ranch riders came in from the back room, and one of them asked who the rider had been who passed through.

'Asked for the Flatbush. Thought you'd know him yourself,' George told him, turning away. Because his back was turned he did not see the glance which flickered between the two.

'Thought the boss said he was taking care of that his own self,' said the one known as Cimarron. 'Maybe we better check that guy. He could be the one we was sent to head off. The hired gun from Santa Fe.'

They finished their drinks quickly and to his surprise, did not order another, making for the door.

He watched them go without regret, and sent a silent prayer for the safety of the girl out at Flatbush. He wished he was capable of doing more.

On the other hand . . .

'Was I you, I'd not be in too much of a hurry to catch up with that guy,' he told the departing backs. They did not hear him, but it might have saved a good deal of trouble if they had.

2

Morgan Fetterman felt good, real good, even if he said so himself, which he did, often. He was a fine-looking man, a wide-shouldered, deep-chested man with a handsome head of red-gold hair, a wide, humorous mouth and eyes which looked as though they would smile easily.

This, like a lot of things about Morgan Fetterman, was an illusion. Things which made Morgan Fetterman smile with genuine pleasure were the things of which nightmares were made.

He was on his way out to the Flatbush at this very moment, accompanied only by his foreman, a man called Lester Black, who had come into the country with Morgan Fetterman some years before. Some said Fetterman came from the east. Others believed equally strongly that he came from the north, and there was a small school of thought which leaned towards Europe. He had the polish, they said, of a Frenchman.

They were all wrong. Fetterman had come from England by way of Canada, where he had teamed up with Lester Black in a prison work party. Like called to like across the rock-pile, and an alliance was formed. It survived the rock-pile and the hideous conditions in the jail, lasted through the jailbreak that brought about the deaths of two prison guards and half a dozen fellow inmates, sacrificed as shotgun fodder, and through the hardships of the Canadian winter as they slogged their way south and across the line.

Behind them they left a trail of murdered people and looted isolated farmhouses and shacks. Things were done on their way south which neither of them could afford to have known, and each survived only because one had decided that if taken he could blame his worst crimes on the other.

In Morgan Fetterman's case there

was always the suspicion, buried at the back of his conscious mind that, in any case, he was never quite sure that he would be quite quick enough to be able to kill his partner before Black killed him.

Black had no such doubts. But he did have the intelligence to realize that he made a lot more money in partnership with Fetterman than he had made by himself. While this continued he was willing to go along with almost anything Fetterman proposed. Fetterman did the thinking, Black the acting. It worked.

Just at the moment they were in perfect harmony. Fetterman wanted the fertile valley of the Flatbush for two reasons.

It was high and enclosed, with easy if narrow entrances at each end and it ran east to west through the range. Above all, it had grass and water, permanent water in a land where streams were periodic and lakes often dried up almost overnight.

There did not seem to be any flaw to

the place. His own ranch, which grew every time he had a mind to grow it, lay to the west and north. He had won the deeds to the original land at a poker table in Wickenburg, and the original owner had disappeared after voicing his objections too loudly while in drink a couple of nights later. It had been a wet period and the Hassayampa river, usually dry, was flowing. People speculated that he had wandered down to the river and fallen in, which was at least a wink and a nod from the truth. In he had certainly fallen, for his body was found when it dried up a few days later, caught on a snag a half-mile downstream.

On the subject of how exactly he had come to fall in, it was not wise to speculate, so they didn't. Not out loud in public, anyway.

Today, Morgan Fetterman had other things on his mind. He was riding a fine horse, a palomino as blond as a dancehall girl. He was wearing light-coloured clothes and a big brown hat with a silver band and a feathered cockade.

He had come to the Flatbush Valley with a set of deeds, which looked very impressive if suspiciously new, which was hardly surprising because he had written the deeds himself. Not all of his time in prison had been spent on the rock-pile, and he wrote a good, clear hand of which the governor made use in his office. A disgraced lawyer also worked in there and they had learned much from one another. The lawyer had learned the ultimate lesson in life which was not to turn his back on Morgan Fetterman, though he learned it too late, and died in the jail-break.

Morgan Fetterman had taken care to learn about his enemy, and what he had learned was that old Jubal Cotton, the owner of the Flatbush, had no mind to sell his ranch. Les Black had taken care of that by following the old man out into the desert when he came to town for supplies and leaving his body in a dry wash, where the remains were eventually found. That left the place in the charge of an old ranch hand and a young woman called Jemima Penrose who, Fetterman supposed, was the cook.

He proposed to show them the deed — assuming either could read — and tell them to pack their things and be gone. They could take a horse each in lieu of pay owing, which he assumed it was. The old man had precious little money on him when he died, and Les Black had taken that. The old man's horse and packmule he allowed to run off and find their own way home, since they would both be known and recognizable, so he could not keep them without attracting attention.

Black was leaning over to examine the side of the trail. After a moment he reined in and dismounted, bending to study the ground.

'What's up?' Fetterman pulled up alongside him but did not dismount. He had learned to let Les Black do the tracking, and getting down and trampling around would only make it harder to read the sign.

Black walked slowly along the road, bending low from time to time to peer at the ground.

'I reckon there's a man ahead of us,' he said, straightening up. 'Horse apple here's still damp. Feel.' He handed a lump of horse dung up to be inspected, covering a contemptuous smile with his hand when Fetterman shied away from it.

'Take your word on it,' he said, hastily. 'So what?'

'You and me don't want no witnesses for what we may have to do,' Black said softly. 'Don't know who this is, up ahead, but if we don't know, he certainly ain't no friend of ours, and that's no lie.'

That was true enough, anyway. Fetterman stood upright in his stirrups and took a long, careful look around. No rider raised the dust on the road, and no strange figure was to be seen on the surrounding countryside. Just the dun-coloured rock and occasional stand of ocotillo, interspersed among the Joshua trees and rock. For the millionth time he wondered why people thought deserts were all sand, when in fact this one at least was covered in spots of green. Dusty green to be sure, but green nevertheless, though all of it scratched or stung or poisoned the unwary.

Oddly, he felt at one with it, because throughout his life he had learned that almost everything in the world — his world, anyway — scratched or stung or poisoned. The way to get along was to scratch or sting or poison fast and first.

'Well, we didn't invite him to the party,' he said. 'He wants to deal himself a hand, he'll have to take his chances and play it. One thing — if this turns nasty, we don't need no eyewitnesses.'

Black shot him a glance under the brim of his hat, and grunted. He had understood from the start. He was just confirming that his partner did. They were here to clear the ranch. If they had to bury the evidence, three bodies would fit into a hole dug for two. At the thought, he drew his gun, flipped open the loading gate and slipped a cartridge into the chamber he normally carried empty under the hammer for safety.

★　★　★

The trail between the entrance to the valley and the ranch house was not long but it was a wonder to behold for men accustomed to the desert.

The grass started at the gate through the mountains. A carpet of grass, sere and brown at first, but shading into green as it swooped down the valley floor to a small lake in the bottom. The lake was fed by a stream, which emerged from a cleft in the valley's steep wall and wound its way past the ranch house and stables to the lake.

Two dams had been built on its course, one a spreader dam which fed water into the grass and turned it a blessed green where there were two large fenced corrals.

The other created a pool under some cotton-woods near the low ranch house, a structure of stone and wood which showed signs of having been added to from time to time by a builder who had both enthusiasm and an eye for the future.

He had an eye for a fight, too. There was no cover for a hundred yards up to the house, there were loopholes in the door and shutters, and a covered way led from the house to the stables. And loopholes in the stable walls as well.

'Ain't a house, that's a fort,' growled Black as they let themselves in to the yard. He looked over the riding stock in the small corral near the stables and grunted approvingly. 'Good stock, too.'

'All mine, now,' agreed Fetterman, and missed the flicker which crossed his foreman's face as he turned towards the house.

There was a big mustang tied to the hitching rail in front of the house, with saddle-bags and a rolled slicker behind the saddle, though the carbine was missing from the saddle's boot. The man whose tracks they had seen along the road was here, but he was not to be seen.

Warily, they rode their horses up to the ranch house. Fetterman swung down, looping the reins over the hitching rail. When he straightened up, he found himself looking at a handsome, dark-haired woman with a strong face and level, green eyes.

'Welcome to the Flatbush, gentlemen,' she said and the low, musical tones of her voice were as big a surprise as her appearance. In a land where women sweltered in corsets and dresses designed for the temperatures of East-coast New York, she was wearing a white open-necked shirt and swirling black skirt held in at her slender waist with a belt of conches linked with chains, which boasted an intricate silver buckle.

On her wrist was a wide, heavy silver bracelet inset with coral and turquoise. Fetterman had seen enough Navajo jewellery to recognize a work of great value. Not something a servant would be able to afford, he knew.

'Howdy, little lady,' he said easily as he walked up to the steps. 'I am Morgan Fetterman, and I am the new owner of this ranch, but I was not expecting to find a lady as beautiful as this to welcome me to my new home. What are we going to call you?'

'You can call me whatever you have a mind to, Morgan Fetterman, but it had better be respectful while you are standing on my land, and you are standing on my land right now. You do not own this ranch, I do. I inherited it from my uncle and if that hand comes out of your jacket holding anything but a handkerchief, you are going to find out that face to face I am as good a shot as my uncle was.'

She paused, and from the cover of the folds of her skirt, her right hand emerged holding a gun. It was a small revolver, but at the range just as deadly as a canon, and to Morgan Fetterman, staring down the barrel, it looked almost as big.

He took his hand very slowly from his pocket, to show that he was holding the deeds to the valley that he had so carefully prepared, and made to step forward and hand them to her.

'I didn't invite you into my house, Morgan Fetterman,' she said, evenly. 'And uninvited guests can easily be mistaken for invaders. Have a care.'

He put both feet back on the ground, controlling his breathing with difficulty, and concentrated for a second on bringing his temper back under control. This woman needed a sharp lesson in manners, and by Lucifer, he was looking forward to giving her one.

'Now see here,' he started. 'No need for firearms here. I have a genuine deed to this ranch — indeed to all this valley. I don't know what your uncle told you but he lost it fair and square in an honest game of poker.'

'My uncle could not play poker. He thought gambling was a sin and never wagered.'

'Then he shouldn't have played with

me, and taken strong drink at the same time, for that's the way he lost it.'

She laughed, a genuine shout of mirth.

'A lifelong teetotaller who could not play cards lost his ranch in a drunken poker game? I don't think so, mister. And neither will any judge in the land. Now, get off my land and get off it right fast, you cheap swindler, or I'll let the puff out of you so fast you'll fall flat.'

Lester Black eased himself forward in the saddle and the harness creaked under his weight as he dropped his right hand towards his gun.

'How you going to get both of us, lady? Best thing you can do is drop that popgun, and try being nice. You going to wish you'd never been born, else.'

For a moment, her attention wavered, and Fetterman grabbed for his gun. The draw was fast and smooth and the Colt was just coming out of the holster when a voice spoke from the corner of the house.

'That's going to be the silliest thing

you ever done, mister. Last thing, too.'

The gun hand stopped in mid-draw, leaving Fetterman crouched ludicrously, as though he had been frozen in an instant.

'Good, that's very good, mister. Let's see if you're as good at putting the gun down. Meantime, maybe your friend better shuck his weapon, too. Looks to me like he could be a man prone to making bad mistakes. Fatal, even, know what I mean? Be a real shame to get shot on account of some other guy's mistake.'

Fetterman began to sweat. There was death in that voice.

'You, the one with a face like a rattler with toothache, unbuckle your gun belt with your left hand and drop it. Easy, now. Good. Now, put your hands on your hat. Lace up your fingers real tight, like you was praying. Which you will be if you got any sense. I purely do not like a man who threatens a lady.'

Without taking his aim off Black, he pointed at Fetterman.

'Now, you, fancy pants,' he said to Fetterman. 'Reach out your gun hand real careful, mister whatever your name is, and drop that gun into that water trough. Or if you reckon you can beat a bullet, try your luck.'

Fetterman could hear Black's breath hissing between his teeth, and knew the man was on the very brink of losing his self-control. There was no way the unknown gunman could miss either of them.

'Keep your hands on your head, Les,' he muttered. 'We'll have to wait till later to get this guy, but we'll get him in the end. Just remember him.'

Aloud, he said: 'You're taking on a real big risk for a wore-out ranch hand. Sure you can handle it?'

There was a ripple of amusement in the voice that answered.

'Oh, I reckon I can handle a man who needs a hired gun to run a young woman off her land, mister. Just what is your name, so I'll know who to look out for, come the time?'

Fetterman drew in a long shuddering breath, and identified himself. As he did so, out of the corner of his eye he caught sight of Lester Black. The man's hands were working their way free from the cramping grip he had been forced to adopt, and his face was rigid.

'Just who are you, mister?' he said tightly.

'Name's Horn. Luke Horn.' There was amusement in the voice when Fetterman looked up, startled.

'Luke Horn? But I — '

'Yeah, mister. Same Luke Horn you hired to clear squatters off your land. Only it ain't your land is it? And this here young lady ain't no squatter, is she? So it won't surprise you to hear I resigned from your employ. I quit.'

He was carrying the rifle missing from the saddle boot in his right hand, butt resting on his hip. The posture looked easy and relaxed but the eyes under the brim of the black hat were anything but casual.

'I hired you to work for me!'

Fetterman exploded. 'You took my money, and now you want to renege on the deal. I'll see you dead for this.'

'Mister, I heard some things about you on my way down here, so I decided to see for myself. Found out what you said in your telegram was a pack of lies, so I quit. Here's your money, less some I took for travel on my way.'

He reached into a shirt pocket and took out a wad of notes with a string round them and tossed them to Fetterman, who caught them.

'Good catch. Real fast. Now we're straight. Get back on your toy horse and ride out of here, now. And tell that tinpot hardcase, if he don't stop wiggling his fingers I'll shoot them off.'

'Nobody's that good a shot!' exploded Black, goaded beyond bearing.

'You'd best pray I am, for the next thing to your fingers is your head. You wanna try for it? I'm game.'

Black however was not. Suddenly his hands, locked on his head, were totally still. The man who called himself Luke

Horn nodded and grinned.

'Good call, mister. You get to live another day. Now get off this land. Next time I see you on it, you're dead men.'

As he spoke, he stepped forward. As he did so a little fountain of dust sprang from the ground where he had been standing. From the nearest clump of cottonwoods by the stream down from the little lake, the report of a rifle sounded a split second later. The palomino, startled by the hornet buzz of the ricochet, started bucking like a mad horse, and Fetterman, caught in the act of mounting, grabbed at the saddle horn with one hand and pitched himself in to the saddle.

Lester Black's hands came off his head as though they had been blasted off. He crouched over his horse's neck like a jockey and slammed home his spurs. The horse ran for the gate, leaving a succession of dust fountains from the trail.

The palomino came down with all

legs braced and nearly unseated its owner, but Fetterman stayed aboard with a feat of genuine horsemanship and horse and rider set out for the entrance to the valley, belly-down and eyes wild.

Another shot came from the cottonwoods and splintered a window in the ranch house. The girl vanished through the ranch house door in a swirl of skirts, and Horn slammed three shots into the cottonwoods. Then he rolled over half a dozen times until he was under the ranch house steps.

'You all right?' called the girl, and was answered with a barrage of swearing. Then: 'Yeah, I'm all right, though I ain't got no right to be. What kind of a dumb-ass am I to think a snake like that would come a-calling with no back-up? Pure-dee dumb, that's me!'

As he spoke, two riders broke from the cover of the cottonwoods and raced for the gorge which marked the entrance to the valley. The defenders let them go without firing.

'We,' said the girl, with acid in her voice, 'have to talk. Just who the hell are you, to start with?'

3

He turned, carefully holstering his gun as he did so, and walked to the horse at the hitching rail to put away his rifle. Her own pistol barrel followed his every step. And he was careful not to make any sudden moves.

'I asked you a question, mister. If I don't get an answer, I am liable to get right testy,' she said. He could see from where he was that the rifle was cocked.

'Name's Horn — Luke Horn,' he said loudly and clearly. 'I'm a hired gun that that rat brought in to get you out of here.' He saw the pistol barrel jerk as he said it and tensed ready to dive for the cover of the water trough, but the threatened bullet never came.

'So what made you change your mind? Didn't he offer enough?'

'Nobody offers enough for a man's

life. Ain't possible to offer enough for a woman.'

She dropped the barrel of her gun until it rested on the rail of the stoop, though he noted that she failed to uncock the hammer into the safe position, and the barrel still pointed at him.

'You better come inside,' she said. 'Out here, we're sitting targets. But try and touch that gun, and I'll kill you.'

He didn't doubt it for a moment, but he tipped his hat over his eyes and allowed her to herd him into the house.

It was a surprise to him. Outside it may have looked like a fort, but inside it was a warm and comfortable place. Navajo rugs hung on the walls, and covered the furniture in colour.

On the rear wall of the big room there was a huge stone fireplace and chimney breast, decorated with historic weapons. He identified firearms two centuries old and swords which must have arrived with the Spanish conquerors of the region far back in the shadows of time, stone axes and flint-tipped arrows, a pair of Indian lances ten feet long with tassels of feathers.

'Your uncle's gear?' he asked, gesturing at them. She nodded.

'He liked the Indians. Some of them, anyway. Pimas and such. Said he even had some admiration for the Apaches, though he never turned his back on them.'

He laughed. 'I think I would have liked your uncle, ma'am. Shame I never got to meet him. Sounds like a right sensible *hombre*.'

'Yet you came here to kill him!'

He shook his head and gestured at one of the chairs.

'Mind if I set, ma'am? I been sitting on that saddle for so long I come near to forgetting what a real chair feels like.'

She nodded her head wearily.

'Sit down, then. But keep your hands where I can see them. I still don't know what you are doing here. When you rode in you were in too much of a hurry to tell me.'

He relaxed into the chair with such genuine pleasure that she almost forgot he was by his own account a hired killer. The thought brought the pistol barrel up again and a hard edge to her voice.

'All right, Horn. You got inside, you like my house, you got to sit in a comfortable chair. Now talk. And make it good. All I know is you came riding up in a heck of a hurry, told me there was trouble on the way, and hunkered down behind the corner of the bunkhouse.'

He took a long cheroot from his inside pocket, cocked an eyebrow at her for permission to smoke, received it and lit up. The perfume of the tobacco was rich in the room.

'Well, now, ma'am, you got a right to call me a hired gun, for that's what I am. But I ain't a hired killer. Not of innocent folks, anyhow. Me, I like to think of myself as more of an enforcer.'

It was a common enough story. Up to the middle years of the War Between the States, he was just a farm boy working away on a hardscrabble farm all the hours God sent just to stay alive. The family did not have time to worry about the war. Survival was their most pressing problem.

And then, one day, the war came to find them.

'We heard there was robbers in uniform around. Guerrillas they called themselves, but they was just thieves and murderers, mostly. You'll have heard tell of Bill Anderson, Quantrell and the Youngers, I don't doubt. Well, there was others as bad both sides of the line. Some of them called on us. I was the only survivor.'

He had buried his family in the field behind the smouldering ruins of their home, and marked the single grave with a single marker. Then he took the muzzle-loading rifle he used for hunting, his water bottle and the blanket which had been least singed by the flames and started tracking the raiders.

He caught up with three of them

within the first two weeks, and armed himself from the weapons he took from their bodies. Then he set out after the rest.

'I joined up with the first outfit I come across, a Yankee unit calling itself Hookey's Volunteers, to try and find them. Never did, though. Trouble was, once they got rid of their loot, I didn't have no way to identify them. End of the war, I was a sharpshooter with Hookey's Union outfit, with no sharp-shooting to do and nobody to tell me how to make a living. Then I heard of a man hiring good shots for a job cleaning up in Georgia, so I signed up with him.'

' 'To the winners belong the spoils', he kept on saying. Well, he sure spoiled plenty. Weren't nothing but a bunch of thieves and bandits, same as the ones burned out my family and put me on the road. One night I got sick to my stomach with what we was doing. I shot the boss and his sidekick, and took to the road my own self.'

But he was stuck with his way of life. The only talent he had to sell was an unerring aim and a fast draw with a handgun. The only way he could live with himself was to examine very carefully the story he was told when he was hired and make up his own mind which side was in the right.

'Often as not I finish up fighting against the man who hired me in the first place,' he said ruefully. 'Don't pay so well, but I gets to sleep better of a night.'

She had to admit that if he had not ridden to warn her, she would have been taken totally by surprise when Fetterman and his foreman turned up, and that the hatred on Fetterman's face had seemed genuine enough as he rode off.

'How did you know Fetterman and Les Black were on their way here?'

He grinned. 'I didn't. Knew that Fetterman said he wanted some squatters cleared off some land he'd inherited, which is what I was hired to do. Called in at the town to get directions, and the barkeep gave me a real mouthful. Made me wonder again about the job, so I come out here to see for myself.'

'Seemed to me I wasn't alone, out there on the trail, so I laid up and watched my back trail.'

'Pretty soon along comes Fetterman and another *hombre* on the trail. I'd heard Fetterman was a pretty fancy dresser and this guy seemed kind of fancy-dressed for a simple rider. This here was the only place he could be coming, so I beat him to it. Good job I did, too. He and that Black guy had you dead to rights. Never let them separate. Splits your attention and your aim.'

'I don't know what you expect of me now,' she said, letting down the hammer of the Winchester. 'I have the ranch, but Fetterman must know there's no money here and I haven't any cash to hire hands even to make a small gather of horses to sell to the army, which was how my uncle used to live.'

He stood up and walked to the window to look out at the ranch.

'Your uncle must have had help. Ranch is well looked after, stock's been branded. Water's clean and the channels are cleared. Who did all of that?'

She nodded. 'Uncle did all the work along with Fed Sauermann as *segundo*. When they needed a round-up for the army they used to hire in riders from north of here. Fed can't do it all by himself, even when I do pitch in and help.'

He turned from the window. 'What does he look like?'

'Fed? He's an old guy, all rawhide and barbed wire, but he works like ten and I'd trust him with my life. Why?'

'Guy like that's just riding in from the west range, and he ain't sparing his mount. Something's up, likely.'

Fed Sauermann came up the ranch house steps like a cavalry charge, and stopped dead when he saw Horn sitting at his ease in the chair. His hand reached for his gun and was only dropped when the girl said quietly: 'It's OK, Fed. Seems like he's a friend.'

The spare cowpuncher took his hand away from his gun, though it seemed to Horn that it moved reluctantly. The old man didn't take his eyes off Horn as he said: 'You know who this is, ma'am? This here's Luke Horn. The gunfighter Luke Horn. Word is that Fetterman sent for him to clear us out of here. You happy about that? 'Cause I sure as hangment ain't!'

The girl said: 'He just ran Fetterman and Les Black off the ranch, and two of the men from the ranch with them. Fetterman wasn't happy. Swore he'd kill Horn, and two hands he brought with him surely did their best. They took a shot at him from that stand of cottonwood up towards the canyon, and they only just missed.'

The argument seemed to have made up her mind.

'I believe you, Mr Horn. We'd be glad of your help,' she said.

Horn stood up and looked at the

cowhand. 'How about you, Sauermann? Don't like to turn my back on a man who can't trust me. Makes me right nervous.'

'And when you get nervous you're like to shoot the wrong man, huh? You don't need to worry, mister. Me, I only shoot people in the front.'

He turned to the girl.

'What I come to tell you was this, ma'am: there's a whole herd of beef coming in from the west pass, and a whole lot of trouble driving them. I seen Alley McCoy, Jule Crown and a third one could have been Fletcher Brittan. Didn't get a clear look at him, though. Then there was another three or four hard-looking men I didn't recognize. Know their kind, though. We got trouble.'

She looked at Horn quizzically. 'You in?' He nodded.

'Go with Fed, then, and see if there's anything you can do. Someone had better stay and watch the ranch, and make sure Fetterman doesn't come back.'

He nodded again.

'If he does,' he said, 'kill him. Don't argue, don't negotiate. Just kill him.'

He turned his back on Fed Sauermann and walked down the steps to his horse. He was mounted up before the cowhand had a chance to get his foot in the stirrup, and when Sauermann did mount up, he waved him on ahead.

'Don't worry,' Horn said when Sauermann threw him a suspicious glance. 'I only shoot 'em in the front, too.'

4

Even before they could see the herd they could see the dust they were raising. Horn and Sauermann could hear them too: the muted rumble of hundreds of hoofs even from the grassy floor of the valley, the curious clicking sound of hundreds of horns knocking together as the tightly bunched cattle moved onwards.

'They're driving 'em tight,' commented Sauermann, and Horn nodded.

'Come across some dry Sonora desert to get here, I reckon,' he said. 'Herders daren't let 'em spread out. Soon as they smell that water, they'll get to running, and they'd lose cows in a stampede. Nobody looks after cattle better than them as stole 'em.'

Sauermann shot him a glance. 'Personal experience?' he asked.

'Sure is. I was in more than one

provisioning raid in the war. Reckon I helped rustle more Southern beef than the Jensen gang and the Hardimans put together. Ate plenty of it, too. Rustled beef tastes better.'

He threw a glance sideways at Sauermann's hardbitten face, rigid with disapproval.

'Don't worry, old-timer,' he said. 'I stopped rustling cows about the same time men in grey uniforms stopped shooting canons at me. Same reason, too.'

'Peace broke out?'

'Peace broke out.'

Sauermann grunted two or three times, deep in his chest. Later, Horn came to recognize it as his version of laughter.

Horn pointed down into the bottom of the valley, where two horsemen had appeared, riding several yards apart. The herd was just coming into sight behind them, tightly packed as he had predicted, and restless as they smelled the grass. Some of them were already making attempts to break away and graze, keeping the outriders busy heading them off and turning them back into the herd.

'Those boys are already having trouble with the herd,' he said. 'Won't take much to get them running. Keep the herders busy, specially if some of them beeves get a whiff of the water up ahead.'

The older man nodded. 'Be another half-hour or more before they get a smell of the water in that lake,' he opined. 'If we get into position now we can get them going a treat by the time they pass Blue Bluff back there.'

He glanced sidelong at Horn. 'Trick you've pulled before, huh?'

Horn was getting mightily sick of the constant ribbing, but he recognized that this was exactly what the hard old man wanted. He pulled his horse round to head down the valley following the herd, about 300 strong, which were by now all in plain sight and beginning to show signs of restiveness. The hands were kept very busy and the strain of keeping the thirsty cattle under control was beginning to show.

He watched as one rider roped a particularly troublesome steer round the horns, but missed the saddle horn when he went to snub off the end of the lariat. The effect when several hundred pounds of angry beef hit the end of the unsecured rope was predictable, and the unfortunate cowboy came out of the saddle as though he had been blasted out of it with mining powder. He travelled several yards through the air before he hit the ground.

Perhaps through stupidity, perhaps because the impact knocked the common sense out of him, he did not let go of the rope at once and the running steer towed him into a stand of cholla cactus. At this he did let go with a howl, and was hopping around trying to pull out the spines when the steer turned on him.

Western cattle might have been wary of a man on a horse but had no respect for one on foot. The steer dropped its head and charged, trailing the lariat behind it. The rustler took one look, stopped worrying about the cactus spines, and showed cattle sense enough not to try and outrun the steer, but doubled back and ran round the cholla in tight circuits.

The lariat, winding round the cholla, brought the steer closer in, and the terrible barbs reached out for it, catching first in the beast's coat, but then in its nose. The steer's weight ripped the cactus out of the ground, but the barbs stuck in the soft part of its nose, driving the beast mad with rage and pain.

Eventually, the rustler got out his gun, dared to go closer to the pain-maddened beast, and shot into it. He must have known what he was doing because he dropped it with the third shot, just as one of his colleagues came up with his horse.

It was only just in time. The herd, already jumpy and irritable, went off like a swarm of monstrous bees. The rustlers, caught by surprise, could do nothing to control it, and concentrated on staying in their saddles and out of the way.

Horn and Sauermann found themselves helpless with laughter and with no job to do.

'All very fine, but why was they bringing them cows here?' Horn said suddenly. 'Can't have been more than a few miles away when Fetterman and Black come up here this morning with their fake deed. Other side of the mountains, there ain't nothing but open country and desert, so they wasn't just passing by this way. They was coming right here, and that is just what they did.'

'Like they knew they'd be able to come right through,' agreed Sauermann thoughtfully. 'Now, how did they know that? The old man ain't been gone more than a couple of weeks, and that beef must have been on its way more than that.'

The answer was waiting for them down on the floor of the valley where the unfortunate rustler had been unhorsed and dragged into the cactus. A hard glimmer among the weeds on the valley floor caught Sauermann's eye and the old man swung from the saddle to investigate. He stood up, swinging a branding-iron.

'Circle C', he said, inspecting it. 'That's Willie Donaldson's mark. He ranches down towards Fort Yuma. Worked there a spell, a few of years back. But that's strange.'

'Why?'

'Willie raises cattle on an army contract. Raises them along the Gila, and sells direct to Fort Yuma. But he don't sell them no place else. Says it takes all his time just to fill the army contract, what with Indian raids an' all. What this lot doing with them?'

Horn reached out for the iron and the old man handed it over. It was no running iron, knocked up hastily at some makeshift forge, but a well-made, professional job, meant for hard use on a lot of cattle.

'But why make an iron as already belongs to some guy?' he asked, curious. 'Could this Donaldson guy be rustling cattle and selling them to the army?'

The old man sucked his teeth dubiously.

'Hard to tell what a man will do if he's hard-pressed,' he said. 'But I'd be surprised, myself. Willie's a tough, hard man. Has to be, where he's ranching. But I'd never see him as a thief. Drive a hard deal, sure. You could lose your back teeth trying to cut a deal with Willie. But what he does comes from in front. He might knock you down and stomp you, but you'd be able to see him a-coming.'

He climbed back on to his horse and went over to the dead steer. It had a newly healed brand on its hip, which obviously came from the same iron. On close examination, it had been fitted neatly over a previous brand, so well that the original was unreadable. He was reaching for the knife on his hip when Horn stopped him.

'Leave it,' he said. 'They'll be back for the meat before nightfall. If they see the hide's been tampered with, they'll know they were seen. We need to get that girl out of the ranch house and to somewhere safe before they find out friend Fetterman's fake deeds didn't work.'

'You mean?'

'This lot has been on its way for days. This ain't no sudden dash. It's been planned, and them cows was aimed at this valley days ago. The fake deeds was just one part of the plan. Fetterman wants this valley and from the look of it, he's willing to do anything to get it.'

He wheeled the horse and Sauermann was just in time to catch up with him as he set out along the valley floor.

'Not that way!' shouted the old man. 'They'll see us easy. Follow me.' He clapped his heels to his horse and led the way across the floor of the valley and into the broken ground on the opposite side.

★   ★   ★

They could hear the cattle all the way on their journey, and occasionally catch sight of them, too. The herd had hit one of the branches which fed the central lake and had spread out along it, drinking. In their parched state, the steers could not have been shifted with cannon fire and the herders seemed content to let them drink and feed. They made no attempt to follow the trail beyond the lake to the ranch house in its dip, made tiny by distance.

'What now?' asked Sauermann as they rested their horses for a few minutes in the cover of a little knoll crowned with aspens. 'Why ain't they at the house? Place is wide open to them, with nobody there but Miss Jemima and the cook.'

'Maybe they got orders to leave things alone?' asked Horn, equally mystified. 'Least it gives us time to get her out of there. Let's go.'

Together they dropped behind the knoll and made their way along the back of the creek towards the ranch house. Dusk was falling, and down by the herd, the cook fires were being lit. The cattle, tired and watered, looked as though they were settling for the night.

It was as peaceful a scene as any campfire minstrel could write a song about.

And it was all hopelessly, insanely wrong.

5

The ranch house was a blaze of lights in the early dusk. Lamps and lanterns glowed in the windows and in the yard.

Within the house there was no sign of movement, though smoke rose from the kitchen chimney and caught the glow of the lamps. The whole set-up was silent except for the occasional stamping of hoofs from the home corral.

The two men walked their horses along the dark side of the creek through the cottonwoods, and dropped from the saddle silently when they were close enough to the house to see in through the windows. There was still no sign of movement though, in the lighted rooms that they could see. No pans clattered in the kitchen, no voices came from the house.

'Don't like it,' said Sauermann predictably as they knelt by the corral.

'I don't like it at all. Ain't like her to have the place all lit up like this. She's careful with the oil.'

Horn agreed with him. There was no movement, but there was also no way to approaching the house without putting themselves in the light, and making themselves a sitting target to anybody waiting in the house or the darkness out beyond the corrals. He said as much to the old cowpuncher.

The old man gave one of his grunting laughs.

'Oh, there's a way in, sure as shooting,' he said. 'Follow me if you've a mind to. This way.'

Crouching, they made their way round the house to the rear where a pile of rocks was half-hidden in the trees. The old man stopped when they approached it, and took off his spurs. Horn, wondering, did the same and wrapped them in his bandanna. Then he followed Sauermann down to the base of the rocks.

Sauermann ducked his head and

vanished into the shadows. There was a grating sound of stone on stone, and a hiss from the dark.

'You coming, or what?'

Horn felt with his hand and found the sides of a space between the rocks. Ducking, he felt his way in and heard the grating again behind him. A match scraped in the darkness, and Sauermann's face grew out of the blackness.

'Look,' he said.

From the inside the door was ingenious: a massive wooden frame in which the stone slab was mounted like a door, but turning on a pivot halfway along the lower edge of the door with another hammered from rough iron at the top. Some former occupier had taken advantage of the natural materials to make an escape route.

'Done this one my own self,' the old man said. 'Passageway was here before. I just put the door on her. Meant to save you from savages — red or white, don't make much difference.'

He took a stub of candle from a hole

in the wall, and used the last gasp of the match to light it, then led on down the passage. It was clear almost immediately that it was a natural fault in the rocks, though it showed signs of human improvement in one or two places, and a couple of natural side passages dived away from it.

'Reckon the old Spanishers started mining down there when they come into the country,' said Sauermann quietly. 'Don't know as they found anything, though. Mining's out of my line. Cows I can handle. Rocks is just rocks to me.'

The passageway was short, and they found themselves under a trapdoor. A short flight of rough stone steps led up to it. Sauermann climbed them, blew out the candle, and put his shoulder to the trap. It lifted easily enough, and a dim light came through the gap.

Horn drew his gun, and eased back the hammer, and together, they crept up the steps.

They were in the rear room of the

ranch house, and what seemed like the only one which was not brightly lighted. In front of them was the outline of the stone fireplace and chimney breast of the building, massive and enduring, and Horn realized that the building itself was very much older than he had thought.

Normally a ranch house this size would be alive with noise. There should be the clatter of pans from the kitchen, the sounds of the rancher and his family moving about and noises from the nearby bunkhouse. Dogs should bark.

Instead there was nothing. The silence was uncanny.

Sauermann pushed the trap wide, and climbed into the room. As he did so, his boot heel slipped from the edge of the trap, and his weight made his step easy to hear.

Instantly, a voice said: 'Reno? That you?'

It was a man's voice, and it came from just outside the alcove which contained the fireplace and trapdoor.

'Uh-huh,' Sauermann said indistinctly. He stepped out of the trap and coughed.

The watcher outside, plainly uneasy, said: 'Any sign of them?' He was not cut out for keeping a silent watch, for instead of staying in hiding until he had confirmed the identity of the intruder, he stuck his head round the corner of the alcove and said: 'Where do you reckon they are?'

'Right here,' said Sauermann softly and rapped him hard on the head with his pistol butt, catching him as he fell. Horn made a grab at the man's gun, but he missed and the weapon rattled across the floor noisily. Together they pitched the man's unconscious body down the trap, but it was too late. Outside the door, another voice sounded.

'Who was that? Can't you keep quiet for ten minutes together? They should be here any moment. Now, quieten down.'

There were agreeing murmurs from

around the house and Horn realized that there had to be at least half a dozen men around, in ambush. Sauermann realized the same and in the reflected light from the next room Horn saw him move as quietly as he could towards the door. As he did so, there was a sound very like a sob from the shadows.

Horn stepped over towards it and found himself staring at a shapeless bundle dwarfed by an old easy chair. The chair was made from a wooden frame and had a leather seat and back. He could see the bundle move and raised his pistol for a blow when a distinctly feminine sob came from it.

Instantly he dropped to his knees and clapped his hand over where the mouth should be. He was nearly accurate but caught the girl's nose a sharp rap, which elicited a muffled and outraged growl.

'Quiet, darn it,' he hissed in her ear. He tried to lift her from the chair, but felt the heavy wooden frame trying to come with her and realized she was actually tied to the chair.

He sheathed his gun and felt along the arms until he came to her bindings, drew his knife and slipped the point between her arm and the chair and cut the ties. They were cruelly tight, and he could hear her breath coming sharply as the returning circulation brought fresh pain. Yet she was still able to use her fingers to undo her own gag. The breath hissed in her teeth as she did it, but that was the only sound.

He found and cut the bonds on her ankles, and helped her out of the chair with the aid of Sauermann, who was back from the door.

The old man silently helped her to the open trapdoor, and let her down through it; there was a muffled groan as he did so. The stunned lookout was coming to.

Together, they hoisted him out of the hole, and laid him out just as the girl had been in the chair. Then both men dropped through the trap and gently lowered it behind them. As it closed they heard another, louder, moan from the chair and a voice from outside called: 'Thomson? That you making noise again? Goddammit, this is supposed to be an ambush!'

The closing trap cut off his words. Sauermann lit the candle stub and led the way back down the passage. They moved as fast as the girl could hobble, and within minutes were at the outside entrance.

The light went out, the slab ground its way open and within minutes they were in the cottonwoods again. With one man in front and the other bringing up the rear, they made for their tethered horses.

★ ★ ★

The first shot was a complete surprise. The muzzle flash lit up the trees and the horses started to plunge and pull at their halters.

'Gotcha!' roared a voice, and the gun banged out like cannon. In the dark and their excitement the ambushers were wasting their lead, though, and the muzzle flashes simply told Horn where to shoot.

'Get her away!' he shouted at Sauermann.

The old man shouted: 'Yo!' though the girl protested wildly. Then they were gone.

With a clear field of fire and no friends around whom he might hit, Horn was back on the territory he knew best, and he revelled in it.

He dropped to the ground and eeled along between the trees until he put himself well off to the side. The ambushers were happily blasting away at something or other — what, he had no idea.

But in the dark the muzzle flashes showed him where they were. Black powder burned bright in the night, and since most men shot from the right hand, their bodies had to be — from his point of view — to the right of the muzzle flash. He might not hit the shooter but he reckoned he would make him sleep real uncomfortable that night.

He laid himself down in a hollow bounded by a tree root and next to a small rock. The two ambushers were still blasting away at random. He drew a careful bead on the furthest one and shifted the weapon slightly to allow for the difference between the flash and the shooter. The would-be ambusher would be a rifle length back and a hair to the right from Horn's point of view, assuming he was using his right eye. The moment the rifle went off, Horn squeezed the trigger lovingly and immediately rolled over three times to his right.

The move took him behind a tree stump and when he had worked the carbine's action, he peered cautiously round its base. One of the rifles was still banging away but the other, the one he had fired at, was silent.

He drew a very careful bead on the remaining muzzle flash and squeezed off his own shot instantly. There was a startled shout and a noisy threshing in the darkness which told him he'd missed, but somebody had a bad night's sleep.

One down, one frightened, he did not know how badly. Time to go.

He wriggled back through the sparse undergrowth, trailing the carbine with him until he came to the edge of the grove. Now he had another problem. No horse, though he had seen plenty in the corral and by now, he knew, there would be several in the barn, which was the only place the ambushers could have hidden them.

They had seen three people emerge from a rock pile and enter the cottonwoods, in the bright moonlight. Did they know about the tunnel? It had been there in its natural form for ever, then modified and included in the old house for decades, maybe even centuries. The Spanish settlers who occupied this land before the Americans moved in from the northwest had plenty of time to build their strongholds and fortify them, too. Coming across a natural tunnel like this one would have given them an excellent reason for building their hacienda right here by the water in this remarkable valley. With a small force of armed men, the place made a natural stronghold.

Which of course was precisely why the rustlers wanted it. A natural stronghold with running water and grass, and an easily defended perimeter.

Trouble was, he was a stranger here and he didn't know where his only allies were.

First, he needed a horse.

The two ambushers would not have walked all the way up from the ranch house. Why would they? No cowboy would be separated from his saddle for that long. They must have been out searching and come across the horses in the cottonwoods. That meant their own mounts must be near by. He had not heard the sound of hoofs, which in turn meant they could be still around.

He put his back against a rock and ignored the temptation to roll himself a smoke. The cottonwood grove was dark in the moonlight, a shifting pattern of silver and black with the night wind bringing him the scents of the land.

Over towards the house there were signs of activity, which ruled out a half-formed plan to try and Indian his way to the corral or stables and sneak a mount from there. The men at the house must have found their unconscious lookout by now, and found that their captive was missing. The sound of shooting from the cottonwoods would have told them where she had gone, so by now they were on their way to check up.

The wind shifted slightly and to the smell of dust and wet reeds from the creek was added the pungent smell of horse. He swung his head and found the source, a pair of mounts standing only a hundred yards away, in plain sight now that he knew where to look in the black-and-silver world of the cotton-woods.

So why were they still there? There had been two men. One he thought he had killed but the other he knew he had not. Was he waiting in ambush? Surely he was not daft enough to be wandering the woods looking for a target?

From the direction of the house came the sound of hoofs. He had to go and he had to go now. Quickly and silently, carrying his rifle at the trail, he slid through the undergrowth until he was standing alongside a tree a few feet from the horses. Both animals detected him and turned their heads towards him as he reached for their reins, and in that moment somebody twenty or so yards away shouted: 'Hey!'

He abandoned caution, grabbed the saddle horn of the nearest horse, picking up the hanging rein in the same gesture, and flipped himself into the saddle, keeping low along the animal's back to minimize the target. The shouter turned into a shooter, and his muzzle flashes flickered in the trees.

There was another shout from down towards the house, and hoofs hammered, down there. It was not far, and they would be here in a minute.

He laid himself along the horse's neck, clutching reins in one hand and carbine in the other, and threw the animal at the stream side of the grove, where there was open ground and space to run.

The approaching riders yelled when they saw the horse break cover and shots came his way but they were shooting uphill in the moonlit dark and from the plunging backs of running horses, and none of the slugs came near him. He clapped his spurless boots to the horse's ribs, and the animal responded surprisingly well.

He swung it away from the hunters, let it have its head, and it ran. He was away — well away, and he looked over his shoulder to see how far away. When he looked to his front, a mounted man was emerging from the trees ahead of him, a black figure in the moonlight, carbine aimed and in action.

He had only time to twist in the saddle to try and bring his own Henry into play, when the first shot went off, and missed. The second took him in the right shoulder as he raised his carbine to shoot back.

The carbine dropped from a right fist suddenly useless at the end of an arm which had turned into a piece of string. He hung on to the barrel with his left, but the impact of the bullet was shocking, a blow which nearly knocked him from the saddle, and only a lifetime of staying on running horses kept him there.

The horseman gave a cry of triumph, working the loading lever for another shot but he misjudged the speed at which Horn was approaching him. Before he could get his weapon levelled again, the careering horse, spooked by all the shooting and shouting, cannoned into him at full speed, once again almost unseating Horn.

The speed of the horse and the impact knocked the man, who was hampered by his gun, out of the saddle. His horse reared away and Horn's mount shouldered past.

Horn knew he was in trouble. He had been shot before, and he recognized the sickening shock of the slug's impact, realized from the instant lack of control in his right arm that the wound was serious. Soon, there would be pain, serious pain, and he was losing blood fast. He could feel it soaking into his shirt and beginning to work its way down his trouser leg.

His gun was on his right hip, where he could not reach it even if he had not needed his left hand for both the horse and the carbine. He had to get away, and find somewhere to hide where he could bandage himself and lie up. Later he could think of a way to get food and water, and a way to find the girl and the old cowpuncher.

Even while he was thinking of all this, the horse was running fast and the sound of the pursuit was fading behind him. If he stayed in the open they would find him, sure enough, so he needed a bolt-hole.

The pain hit, then. A solid, unrelenting claw of agony. It tore a raw grunt from his throat, and it embarrassed him. He concentrated on staying on the running horse and steering it to the best of his memory back towards the mountains.

6

First there was the sound of water, somewhere near by. He lay and listened to it for a while, curiously content not to move, while memory came sneaking up from the depths of his mind and opened like a cactus bloom on the morning of the single day of its life.

He had been shot. He could remember the shock of the slug hitting him somewhere on the right side of his body. He stayed on the horse because he had to. The image came back to him of the man who had shot him, black in the moonlight with the muzzle flash of his rifle startlingly bright.

With the memory came the first twinge of feeling from his right shoulder, a dull ache which seemed to come from the very bone itself, and which did not fade away. He had been shot before, and he knew the pain would be with him for a long time. He might as well get used to it.

Carefully, he rolled his head first to one side and then to the other. The light was gentle, reflected from somewhere outside.

Outside what? He raised his head gingerly, and took a longer look. The light was dappled and shifting, reflected on a huge stone slab over his head. Towards his feet, which were wrapped in blankets, it was brighter, and the sound of running water came from down there.

To his right and left there was stone, a stone roof over a sandy floor. He could smell the scent of ashes nearby, fresh ashes but not at the moment live ones. There was no smoke.

He shifted again to see further and was punished by a shaft of pain from his shoulder, which made his head swim. He gave a low moan and instantly heard a sharp movement from somewhere else in the cave, and the girl's voice said: 'Luke? You awake?'

He tried to reply but all that came out was a dry croak. Suddenly she was bending over him from behind his head, asking if he was thirsty.

Again the croak, and she was holding a cup to his lips and letting him sip, sparingly, a drink of cold water. It was delicious, and he wanted to gulp at it and never stop gulping, but she took it away again after a couple of mouthfuls.

'Easy,' she warned. 'You've been unconscious for days, and we had to drip it into you. Try and drink too much and you'll spew. There's plenty of it, and you can hear it running. Take it a little at a time.'

He knew she was right and in any case he was as weak as a kitten and could not argue with any strength, so he lay back in his blankets and let her feed him with miserly amounts. Even at this rate he felt like a newly wetted sponge.

'Like some soup?'

Like it? She'd be lucky to get her hand back if it came too close. She disappeared, and there was the sound of pouring, then she was back.

'It's cold, I'm afraid. We don't light the fire in daylight because of the smoke. Up here the air's clear, and we might as well post signs. Here, try it.'

Hot or cold, it was just what he needed. Rich and tasty, it slid down his throat, though she rationed it as she had the water.

While he rested she answered his questions. Yes, she and Fed Sauermann got clean away, but she was worried about him being left behind. They circled back in time to see him shot. The shooter seemed to have been unhurt by his fall front the horse, and had recovered his mount, though he climbed stiffly aboard. By this time, Horn had disappeared into the night. Jemima kept her eye open for signs of pursuit while Sauermann caught up with the running horse and secured Horn aboard.

'He was running out of wind by then, anyway,' explained Jemima. 'We brought you on up here to the line shack. So far as we know, nobody knows about it but us. But we keep a day-long watch. Just in case, and Fed's on watch now.'

It did not look much like a shack to him and he said so. She giggled.

'No, it doesn't. But that's what we call it all the same. We're way above the valley here, to the south side. Have to be careful not to skyline ourselves, but otherwise we're well out of the way.'

She was still talking in her low musical voice when he fell asleep, and it was the first thing he heard when he regained consciousness. It was dark, and a low fire was glowing further back under the slab. There was a smell of roasting meat and a tantalizing odour from a coffee pot in the embers.

'Hi. Glad to see you're awake.' Sauermann was bending over him with a mug of coffee in his hand. He reached forward to hand it over, then paused, embarrassed, when he realized that Horn could not take it in his right hand.

'Give it here!' Horn reached out with

his left and swore when he felt the heat of the tin cup. But his need for coffee was such that he hung on to it and burned his mouth as well, swigging the scalding liquid.

'Careful,' warned the old cow-puncher. 'Some of it's going into your mouth.'

Horn glowered at him and wiped his mouth with the back of his hand.

'Can't bring myself to spill it all,' he explained. 'Gimme more.'

He was halfway through the second cup before he thought to ask about the girl. She had been sitting by his head when he woke up the first time, he remarked.

'Two days ago,' agreed Sauermann. 'You was giving us some troubles back then, so she wouldn't leave you alone. Did her sentry-go and then came down to sit with you. You give her a right hard time, too.'

'I'll apologize later,' Horn told him, watching as the old man reached out of his sight towards the fire and came back

76

with some smoking meat on a skewer. It turned out to be venison with some herbs, and he chomped happily on the chunks for a while. He had intended to eat the lot but was surprised after a few cubes to find he could take no more.

'Full?' The old man grinned, took back the food and started to eat it himself. 'What d'you expect? We been pouring soup into you for more'n a week, and that weren't going down too good, neither. You need to feed up, boy. But slow.'

Horn knew he was right, but the effort of waking and eating had drained him. He felt desperately thirsty, too, and the shoulder was a deep, aching throb. Unconsciously, he touched it with his left hand. Sauermann's beady eye noticed the gesture.

'Paining you? I need to take a look at it. Lay back, now.'

Filled with misgivings, he did as he was told and was surprised to find the old man was gentle and deft with the bandages. He lifted them off, and took a quick sniff at them, nodding as he did so.

'Stopped smelling days ago, but you can't be too careful,' he muttered. 'You heal fast, son. Yonker like you should heal quick and clean, and you have. Just put this over it for the moment. The other bandages won't be down directly, not until Jemima comes down.'

'She washing them?'

'Nope. She's wearing 'em. You gone through three layers of petticoats this last ten days, and that young lady is beginning to look kinda chilly on these cold nights. You should bleed less.'

Horn couldn't find a good argument against this, so he kept quiet. The old man busied himself cleaning a gun, wiping off the barrel, and pulling a hank of scrap material through the barrel on a line.

'You are a plain puzzle to me, boy,' he said as he worked. He raised the rifle so that the firelight would reflect down the barrel, and used his thumbnail as a reflector.

'Me? How come?'

'I had you down as a plain, hard contract killer. Pay the money and name the target, and you'd just come around and bang! Gimme the gold.'

'How do you know I'm not?'

The bright, beady eye ran over him again, considering, then Sauermann shook his head.

'A contract killer wouldn't have come with me to get her. A hired killer wouldn't have given her his horse and stayed back to keep them off her back while she ran for it. How d'you get into this line of work, son? A killer you ain't, and that's for sure. So before you get yourself up off them blankets, what makes you pretend you are?'

There was a silence broken by the snapping of the sticks burning in the little fire. Horn reached out his coffee cup and the old man refilled it, with a firelit grin which made him look like a fiendish carving.

Horn sipped, and laid himself back on the blankets. He was more tired than he had ever been in his life, but somehow he felt a need to talk, and talk he did.

'My pappy didn't hold with the War Between the States,' he said. 'We boys felt different. Felt like a man should come when his country calls and our country was calling loud enough, for sure.'

Trouble was, it was calling with two voices, each of which seemed to represent freedom of one kind or another. But only one of them supported slavery.

'Didn't really make no difference. Israel and me, we wasn't going off to leave Pa alone with Ma and Tillie. Who would have got in the crop? So we stayed and we worked the land.'

Then one day the war came to them.

Horn had taken the horses down to the river to wash them down and water them after the long day. He sat on a log and watched them standing nose to tail in the shallows, cooling their hoofs. Eventually, he gave in to temptation, stripped off and dived in himself.

Ears full of water and his own splashing, he heard nothing. It was the horses who alerted him to the raid. Suddenly one head came up and then the other. Both animals turned their heads homeward.

Then he heard the sounds. The pop-pop of shots filtering down through the woods, the faint yells.

He was on his horse in a flash, cursing himself for leaving his rifle at home. The big draught horse pounded up the hill from the river like a colt, but it was still too late.

By the time he got up to the house it was all over and the raiders were gone. The bodies of his father, brother and mother were strewn around the yard, shot and abandoned. The house his father had built for them was afire, and it was not until the remains had cooled, a day later, that he found his sister's bones among the ashes.

He buried his family in neat, carefully marked graves in a little plot he knew would be overgrown by the summer. He made himself a pack from the blankets the raiders had unaccountably left in the stable which, once again unaccountably, they had not bothered to burn. As a result, his rifle was also preserved, wrapped in a blanket in the tool bin.

He retrieved a skillet from the ruins and cut a slit in one of the blankets for a poncho.

And he went to war.

'Found the first of them in a little town called Shebaville just a few miles away,' he said. 'Simple enough. He was wearing my Pa's coat.'

He recalled clearly the expression on the raider's face at being challenged by a gawky boyish figure carrying a rifle in the middle of the busy bar room. The boy's cloths might be homespun, but the rifle was another matter altogether. Clean, polished and lightly oiled, it did not waver by a hair's breadth.

'Where did you get the coat, mister?'

In the silent room, he spoke with a normal voice, but there was not a man there who did not hear the question, or hear the curdled malice in it.

'Coat?' The raider's eyes were all over the room, but there was no sympathy to be found. Raiders ranged behind the lines, where even the dirt-poor farmers were victims of choice.

'Coat.'

'Bought it fair and square. A week ago, maybe more. What's it to you?'

'So you'll know what's lettered inside the collar, there, left-hand side, right?'

From the expression on the man's face, he did not even know there were letters inside the coat. He started to reach for the collar to look, and stopped because with one stride the boy had the rifle muzzle in his face. The barrel gouged his cheekbone and he froze like a ten-day corpse.

'Mister? You. The gennelman with the derby hat?'

The gambler at the nearest table was a fancy dresser, and his grey derby hat was the least noticeable of his garments, but it was the only one in the room. He raised it and said: 'How can I help you, son?'

'Go round behind this guy and help him off with that coat. Don't get between me and him, for if he tries anything, I might have to shoot.'

'And that rifle would shoot through me, right?'

'You, him, the bar and the wall beyond. Time's a-wasting and my arm's getting right tired. Maybe less trouble just to kill the murdering bastard. Apologize for my rough words, ma'am,' he added for the benefit of the girl at one table. The girl, accustomed to bar room language which would have stripped paint, thought he was sweet.

But the diversion gave the robber the chance he needed, and he grabbed for his gun.

Luke Horn pulled the trigger and the long rifle fired, as he had promised, through the man's head, then through the bar, the wall behind it and into the alleyway between the buildings.

The gambler grabbed for the rifle muzzle, and wrenched the weapon, trying to get it away.

Horn hung on to the butt and, in the struggle to get it, kicked the gambler in the knee. A man behind Luke wrapped his arms round his body and pinned him fast.

Luke found himself on his back on the floor, with half a dozen guns pointed at him, when a voice bellowed: 'Hold on, there! What the tarnation's going on in here?'

The crowd parted to show a short, thickset man in a frock-coat and fancy waistcoat waving a sawn-off shotgun. His face was very red, and he was chewing a cigar which had seen better days. Quite a lot of better days.

'I asked a question!' he bellowed. 'What in tarnation — ?'

He was swamped by an entire saloon trying to get its version in first and silenced it by blowing a hole in the roof, to the fury of the saloon keeper.

Horn managed to get his voice heard in the silence which followed.

'That man killed my ma and pa and I can prove it!' he shouted, and got the attention of the whole room.

'Look in back of the collar!' he said. 'There's a blue flower there and the initials ZH. My ma made that there coat for my pa last winter. She put her initials in everything she made, and a forget-me-not. He was wearing it three nights ago when we got raided. They didn't leave no survivors.'

There was a silence. Men exchanged long looks.

'Stitching's there, all right,' reported the sheriff after a careful look inside the dead man's coat. He stood up, wiping his hands.

'How many, son?'

'Four,' said Luke Horn, climbing to his feet. 'My Ma, my Pa, brother Israel and my little sister. Tillie wasn't but eleven.'

'How come you survived?' asked the gambler, who had been very close to the rifle when it went off, and whose knee hurt a lot.

'Taken the horses down to the river to drink. It was near a mile downhill, and I didn't get back until it was all over. Spent the next day burying my family. Then I taken up the trail.'

He had been on it ever since. But it started that day in Shebaville.

They had treated him well enough. The livery stable, to his surprise, bought the two draught horses and sold him a good mustang, throwing a saddle into the deal which had been left against a debt. He was riding both still.

Of the remaining three men he tracked down two, each leading him to the next, until the trail to the final one snuffed out. He had joined — ironically — another group of irregulars for a while, and finished the War as a sharpshooter, picking off Confederate snipers in a dozen minor encounters.

'End of the war, I was like a whole raft of men. I done nothing in my life but hardscrabble farming and shooting.

Farm was gone, and I couldn't have worked her by myself even if I had a mind to.'

'So you became a killer?'

'What else had I been for years? Soldiers kill folks. Make a man a general, and he gets medals and cheers. Make him a sharpshooter and he gets sneers. Who killed most folks in them years — me or Sherman? He gets honours, I get nothin'. I lost my home, my folks, my brother, my sister.

'Sure, I hire my gun out. I got nothing else to sell. Some folks need my help. Towns want bad men seen off and the sheriff needs help. Ranchers can't handle rustlers all alone. Me, I never killed nobody who wasn't trying like billy-be-damned to kill me, or run out some nesters, or steal cattle, or take somebody's land.'

He raised himself on one elbow and looked her straight in the eyes.

'Your land, for instance, ma'am. Somebody's trying to steal your land. I like you. I like this valley. I even like this old blend of rawhide and vinegar.'

'Don't call me a hired killer, ma'am. You ain't hired me. I come free. But if I have to, I'll kill for you, and we both know I will have to. Them *hombres* come calling on you, the ones tied you up, the ones as shot me, they're the same kind of lowlife took my land and my family. Them, I'll shift for free, little lady, and the world'll be a cleaner place for it.'

She leaned closer to him and stared hard into his face in the firelight.

'One of your eyes is blue and the other one's brown,' she said. 'I hadn't noticed before.'

7

'They're making theirselves right to home. Too darned cosy down there,' Horn reported a week later. He had been celebrating the repair of his right arm by going out for a day's scouting in the valley, and what he saw had confirmed his fears.

The rustlers had taken the place over completely, and the manner of the occupation told him this was no running raid. They were here to stay and they made no secret of it.

There were horses in the corrals at the ranch house and the building was busy with comings and goings. A blacksmith's shop had been set up in the end of the barn, and horses were regularly reshod there. Smoke came from the ranch kitchen chimney. More cattle had come in during the time he had been laid up, and branding fires burned regularly on the range.

'We're turning into the kind of ranch my Pa always dreamed of,' Jemima complained across the fire. 'Cattle everywhere, hands branding, herds coming in and going out. And it's all owlhoot cattle.'

Horn agreed with her. Instead of being run on the usual rawhide lines of an outlaw camp, the ranch was a thriving business.

'We just got to convince them this is not a good idea,' he said. 'Who's the best local law here? And where?'

Jemima rolled her eyes in the firelight. 'You likely saw him when you came through town,' she said tersely. 'Fat man with a rusty vest and bad breath. Gives the law a bad name. Says his name's Bark Pulse.'

'Must have missed him,' Horn said. He accepted a twig loaded with meat from the old cowman, and tore off a mouthful with his teeth.

'Ain't much we can do about it without the law, and law we ain't got,' said Sauermann from across the fire. 'So what else you got in mind?' His bright, beady eye watched Horn over the rim of his cup.

'Well, like you say, we ain't got the law. So we'll just have to think of something else,' agreed Horn indistinctly through a mouthful of meat. 'Hey, where d'you get this here beef? Seems like Mexican fighting bull to me. Tough, hard and not quite dead yet.'

'If you don't like it, don't eat it,' said the old man grumpily. He had killed a calf for the beef and nearly got caught by a pair of patrolling rustlers. He'd had to carry the carcass back to camp over his saddlebow, its blood soaking into his jeans; he was aware he smelled like a slaughterhouse, and was attracting more than his fair share of flies.

'Oh, it tastes just fine. Just won't stop fighting back,' admitted Horn.

'So what do you men suggest?' asked Jemima. 'They aren't going to keep my ranch, that I can guarantee. Not this side of doomsday.'

'Be a pity if some of them cows come up missing,' said Horn. 'Right aggravating, that kind of thing can be. You ever done any rustling, Fed?'

The old man looked up so quickly that Horn knew he was right. He concealed his grin behind his bandanna, and pretended he had not noticed.

'You know this valley better than anyone, Miss Jemima. There any place we could hide, say, a hundred head for a while?'

She rested her arms on her knees and stared at him with calculating eyes.

'There is, but it will take all three of us and even then we'll be pretty short-handed. How are you with heights?' she asked.

'Me? I'll fall off my own boot heels on a bad day,' he said. 'What's the plan?'

Sauermann sat up suddenly.

'You ain't thinking of tasking them over Dead Man's?' he said sharply. 'Oh no! You know what that trail can do even to a few head. If one panics you can lose the lot and your own self as well. You'd have to be loco just to think about it!'

But Horn could tell from her face in the firelight that, whatever Sauermann might say, before he, Horn, was very much older he was going to find out what Dead Man's was and why it made Sauermann's eyes go funny.

★ ★ ★

He was right on both counts.

Jemima led the way the following morning in the grey light of dawn, down to the floor of the valley and along under the rocky wall, keeping out of sight of the ranch house which was several miles away, and tucking them into the side canyons when she could, until she suddenly pulled up and dismounted.

To their valley side there were tumbled rocks the size of houses, chunks of mountain which had detached themselves years before and fallen to the valley floor. On the opposite direction, the south mountain wall climbed away, sheer and riven with canyons and gashes. Underfoot there were tumbled stones which had packed down hard and firm. The horses' hoofs rattled the upper layers of it but the base stones were so tight-packed that they did not shift at all.

Horn dismounted and stared at the wall of rock. It was the usual sandy colour as though some giant child had deserted his building blocks in his sandpit and gone off to play some place else.

Jemima took a swig from her water bottle and pulled her bandanna up over her nose and mouth. Catching his eye, she gestured for him to do the same.

'Dust,' she explained indistinctly through the cloth, and he obediently covered his own nose and mouth, and pulled his hat down over his eyes. Glancing sideways, he saw Sauermann doing the same without being told, and realized the old man was familiar with this route whether he liked it or not.

'Follow me,' the girl said, and, leading her horse, she stepped past one of the boulders along the base of the mountain face.

He did as he was bid, and found the bulge outside the cliff face was not a fold in the mountain but a separate pillar of rock. Behind its flat mass, a canyon opened into the cliff face.

The face itself was not very impressive. A flat surface with the canyon cleft into it as though with a gigantic felling axe. Inside the canyon mouth the floor rose at a gentle angle and as soon as his boot hit the slope he knew why she had advised him to cover his nose and mouth. The dust, fine and clinging, rose up around him in a loving embrace.

Ahead of him the girl walked as though enveloped in smoke, sometimes revealed by the shifting air currents, at others invisible in the cloud. He trudged after her, surprised by how easy it was to walk in the stuff, while at the same time finding it hard to breathe. He sucked air through the bandanna thirstily, trying not to notice the dust that filtered through with it, and trudged on.

Strangely, the dust did not appear to affect the horses which followed along placidly, their hoofs muffled by the dust underfoot.

Then suddenly, they were out of it. The dust fell away, as though they were climbing out of water, and the ground underfoot was rock.

The girl stopped and slapped away at her clothes, raising a cloud of dust once again, and not making very much difference to her appearance. Horn grinned and pulled off his bandanna but didn't bother with the slapping. Sauermann, appearing beside him, looked like the oldest ghost in the world, and Horn told him so.

'Yeah, and you got different colour eyes,' the old man said drily. 'Ain't nobody perfect.'

Ahead the canyon climbed away from them, wide and steep. The trail followed the bottom of the slash through the rocks, but further on up, Horn could see it no longer. The canyon seemed endless.

'Where's the trail?' he asked, and saw the ghost which was Sauermann twitch a grin straight from the graveyard.

'I'll show you,' the girl said and stepped into the saddle, raising her own little cloud of dust. She urged the horse ahead — though up the side of the canyon instead of along the bottom.

Wondering, he followed her and suddenly realized they were on a fold of rock which followed the side of the canyon instead of the bottom. The climb was not steep, and the trail was wide enough to take several cows abreast.

But it had no edge. The outside of the rock shelf simply stopped on a slight outward slope. To herd even a few steers up the ledge the herders would have to ride on the outside of the cattle, next to the drop. Even down here at the bottom of the climb, it was a frightening prospect, but as his eyes followed the trail upwards, he felt himself swallowing convulsively more than once.

'You said you don't like heights, Horn,' said the girl. 'How do you feel about this one?'

'Sick, ma'am,' he said. 'Sick right down to the toes of my boots, and that's no lie.'

'So we'd better try some place else, you reckon?' He could feel Sauermann's eyes boring into him like drills and realized the old man was desperate for him to say yes.

'Is there any place else?'

She shook her head slowly, dislodging a little fall of dust from her hat brim.

'Not that I can think of.'

He took a deep breath and urged the horse forward up the trail.

'Then we better get to it, ma'am. Ain't got too much time, have we?'

★　★　★

99

They made camp in the valley near the entrance to the trail, and ate a sparse supper before turning in for a few hours. Horn took the first watch and was sleeping peacefully when Sauermann roused him in full moonlight.

The horses were saddled. He held his boots upside down and banged them together to make sure nothing had taken refuge in them during the dark hours, then stamped his feet into them with enthusiasm when he was sure he was alone in there.

The girl was chuckling as he hauled himself into the saddle, deliberately using his right arm to get it used to working again. He asked her testily what was so funny.

'We came down here to find some cows to steal, and they just brought us a whole herd,' she said. 'Look.'

He peered over the rock and found she was right: the meadow at this end of the valley held around a hundred head of longhorns.

'Reckon we can shift that many?' he

asked. In the moonlight her face looked like a silvered statue with the devil in its heart.

'If we can't take them with us, we can sure as shooting spread them all over the landscape,' she said. 'Make them earn their money rounding the lot up again. They'll probably think one of their own people did it.'

They probably would, too. Fetterman and his crew had not heard a thing of the rightful owner of the valley — not surprising, since she had been nursing Horn and it had taken all that time for his arm to start healing. Some of the rustlers using the valley probably did not even know of the existence of the rightful owner and her friend.

If beef went missing in a rustlers' hideout, it would seem logical that the thieves were themselves rustlers. Particularly if there was mistrust already. Dishonest men found it easy to believe that other men were dishonest, and here of course, they were.

He grinned to himself and joined the

other two as they filtered into the edge of the herd, and started them gently moving towards the hidden entrance to Dead Man's Canyon. The steers were reluctant to move at first, but having the horses among them got them on their feet, and once some started towards the canyon, the rest slowly followed on.

He was heading off a rebellious one from a cleft between rocks when he heard a startled oath, and a man rose up from beside the rock, right in front of the horse. He was holding a Winchester, but he had clearly been asleep and awakened by the self-minded steer, for he stood staring at the moving herd for a few seconds before he realized it was being driven.

With another oath he flung the rifle to his shoulder, and Horn hit him over the head with his Colt. The man went down like a paper sack in a rainstorm, and the rifle clattered noisily among the rocks.

But his appearance worried Horn.

He was a sentry, and if the rustlers thought they needed sentries in this enclosed space, they expected trouble. If they expected trouble, it was likely they had posted more than one sentry. So where was the other?

He dismounted, struck a match on his thumbnail and examined the rustler. The man was red-headed, deeply unconscious, and breathing noisily, but alive. His gear was tucked into a crevice under the rock, along with a worn saddle, and it included a branding iron with the end bent over to make a straight line.

A running iron, in fact, which could be used in skilled hands to reproduce or modify almost any brand. He had seen men hang on the evidence of having a running iron in their gear, and he knew it was a dangerous thing to possess. On the other hand, there was a germ of an idea in the back of his mind, and a running iron would come in very useful, so he tucked it into his blanket roll and tied the thongs tight.

He sent the wandering steer to join its family and dropped back to the floor of the valley. The logical place to put the second sentry would be the other side of the herd. So he should have sounded off by now.

The girl cantered over to him, to ask what he had been doing and he told her his suspicions. She rose in her stirrups and looked around the moonlit landscape carefully. She was worried but still determined.

'Can you see him?'

He shook his head, realized she could not see his gesture in the gloom and said, 'Nope. And we won't see him until he moves, not in this light. Bothers me we ain't heard from him so far. His friend was up and ready to blast off right away.'

'Friend?'

'Tell you later, but the sooner we can get these beeves into the canyon, the better we're going to be. This silence makes me right nervy.'

'But you're accustomed to stealing cows,'

she said. 'You should be be used to it.'

'I got kinda used to being shot at in the War Between the States, too. Just never got to like it. Get them dogies moving, ma'am. I'll hang back a mite. We may need a rear guard.'

He wheeled the horse and drifted across the rear of the departing herd. The canyon had already boxed in and the cattle had nowhere to go but forward once they were in the rocky cleft.

The second sentry did not appear until the very last of the animals were filtering into the rocks, with the girl behind them to push them onwards. Then he grew out of the dying moonlight, a shadow upon a shadow, surprisingly on foot, and carrying his rifle across his chest.

Horn sat on his horse in the shadow of the rock pillar that marked the entrance to the canyon and almost missed the man until he was close by. The stalker was just as startled to find himself near Horn, but his reaction was surprising.

'Fletch, that you?' he called in a low voice. 'What the hell's going on here? Where's the herd gone? She didn't come past me, that's for certain. Who's moving the stock and where to — and before we done the brands, too?'

Horn replied in a grunt, and prepared to shoot, but the sentry was going on.

'It's them Broken Z boys, ain't it? I didn't like the way they faded their stock into the best place by the water. Those guys got the most takin' ways in Arizona, I swear. I never trusted that sidewinder Black. Seems too keen by a long chalk to get us all to bring our stock here to this valley where it's kind of convenient for him, I reckon.'

He probably had a lot more theories, too, but at that moment, the dying moon picked out Horn's figure in silver and the sentry realized he was not talking to his own colleague. He swore explosively.

He would have been a lot better advised to get his rifle into action, but he missed his chance and Horn's gun butt knocked him out, though not before he could fire a shot.

In the confined space among the rocks, it sounded like a cannon, and to Horn's surprise, it had hardly faded away, leaving him with ringing ears, than another sounded only a little distance away, and a third more remotely.

It sounded as though an attack was taking place all along the line of the valley, and before it could get any further Horn spurred the horse through the gap and up the trail behind the departing cattle.

He caught up with them before they had passed through the dust bowl. He did not realize he was so close until he almost rode into the girl, who was riding drag and making heavy weather of it. The steers at the back of the herd were not keen on the dust, and kept balking at it, but an extra rider swinging a heavy coil of rope at them speeded them up and they went on up the canyon in the dark.

8

He had been right. It really was no place to try and drive cattle, he told himself, swearing bitterly as he rode up the trail in the dark with a crowd of jostling cattle on one side and 1,000 feet of air in the other.

Despite his cattle raids in the War Between the States, Horn had never been at his best with cattle and he was the first to admit it. Horses, yes. His father had always said Luke was a man could take his horse to a prayer meeting and make it sing in tune. He had been tempted to try it at least once, but his father's belt was long and his temper short, so he had thought the better of it.

Now he was cajoling his horse up the trail, flanking the cattle and praying the horse would not slip. Sauermann was acting as trail boss since he was a cattleman to his bones, and Horn and

Jemima were the trail hands. Jemima, Horn had to admit, was better than he was.

His damaged right arm slipped out of its sling for the tenth time, and he hooked it back in the leather without letting go of the reins. It was a curious injury, for it seemed only to have affected his gun hand. The arm itself worked all right, though it tended to ache more and more as the day went on. The way to relieve it was to support it in a loop of leather that he hung from his neck.

It had worked hard today and it felt tired and ached deep down to the bone. He held the reins in his right hand which the sling held in front of his chest in what was within a whisker of the place he would have held them anyway. It freed his left hand to work.

A steer balked at a rock on the road in the dark and shouldered its neighbour towards the edge of the trail. He half saw the bulk move, urged the horse forward and slapped the erring steer across the nose with his coiled rope. It ducked back into the column.

He was surprised when he looked at how far they had come. He could see dimly in the starlight, though only to distinguish light from dark and moving bulk from rock. The hellish part of the pass was almost over and ahead the trail ducked to the left and away from the precipice, following the curve of the breast of the pass and dropping towards the hidden meadows in the valley beyond.

Dead Man's Pass was designed by nature to be used by rustlers. After the terrifying climb out of the valley, and the sickeningly perilous eyebrow trail, it dropped, following the line of the cliff face and ducked through another gap in the cliffs into a small, enclosed valley with a seep at the bottom. There were some ponderosa pines along the foot of the cliffs, and somebody at some time far in the past had built a stone wall across the face of a rocky overhang. There was room behind the wall for several men to roll in their blankets and a smoke stain up the wall at the back showed where whoever had built the place had built his fire. It was a shelter but nothing else.

Sauermann rode ahead to turn the leading steers though the side canyon and into the refuge. The rest followed obediently, glad to get away from the drop. Horn noticed the eye of one of the steers on him as it went past and was reminded that a longhorn steer might be a beef on legs, but it also had the heart and disposition of a cougar and several feet of razor sharp horns which could unseam a man like a cavalry sabre.

He treated them with the respect he would have given a grizzly bear and remembered the steer which had dragged one of the rustlers into the cactus.

When they turned into the valley the steers smelled the water. They needed no herding, and their new owners let them go. Sauermann and Jemima lined up with Horn and all three sat together at the entrance, looking back down the pass. It was a frightening thought that they had come up that dark fold in the rocks in the darkness.

'Where does the rest of the canyon go to?' asked Horn idly. A lifetime of watching his back had instilled a need to know what was around him.

'Round down into the rocks. There's a hole down there goes down to hell itself for all I know. Makes a hell of a noise anyways, when the wind's in the right direction. Give a change in the wind, and you'll hear it from up here. Sounds like the damned, crying.'

There was a note in his voice when he said it which made Horn look at him sharply, and realize the old man had a genuine dread of the place. He dropped the subject, but made a mental note to go and look at it when he got the chance.

★　★　★

They watered their horses and un-saddled and hobbled them, putting their gear in the walled-off cave. Jemima got a coffee pot going and slapped thick steaks into a skillet. The smell of food filled the cave.

'I'll take first watch,' Horn told them. Sauermann might be whipcord and steel through and through, but he was also an old man and he had worked hard for nearly eighteen hours without a break. He did not protest. He took his blankets and rolled into a cocoon at the end of the cave with his head on his saddle and his hat over his eyes, and was instantly asleep.

The girl began to protest but her eyes betrayed her by falling shut halfway through. Horn tucked her blankets round her and let her sleep.

He was deathly tired himself, but he propped himself against the outside wall of the place where he could see down into the shadowy valley. He reloaded both his Colts.

Below him in the valley the herd settled down. It was peaceful, and suddenly he hankered after a life along the same lines. It occurred to him that he liked this place and he had for the first time actually enjoyed working the cattle. He had never felt it before during the war when he was driving stolen Confederate beef under the command of a former rancher turned US Army rustler.

There was a touch at his elbow and he smelled the scent of womanhood close to him.

'My watch,' she said quietly. 'Go sleep a while. I'll rouse Fed when it's his turn.'

But hardly had he laid down his head than someone was shaking him, it seemed. He sat up and realized it was Sauermann and that it was early light. He had been asleep for hours, then. He opened his mouth, but Sauermann laid a finger across his lips and hissed quietly.

'Someone out there, with the cattle,' he breathed. 'Can't see nothing, but the sun'll be up in a few minutes. Could be Indians.'

Indians up here meant Apaches and they were bad news no matter where they were. If they realized the white men had a woman with them they would be impossible to get rid of without a pitched battle.

He reached out, picked up the Henry and rolled out of his blankets. He shook his boots out and hauled them on, then slid silently out of the shelter to where the girl was hunkered down behind a pile of rocks, rifle in hand.

'Where?' he breathed in her ear, and she pointed downhill. In the growing light, he could see that the cattle were on their feet and uneasy. They were all looking the same way, towards the other side of the water hole, which he could just see in the growing light.

'Seen anything?'

She shook her head. 'No, but the cows can see or hear something. Look at them.'

There were field glasses in his saddle-bag. He eeled back, careful not to show himself above the stones, and brought them out. Through them he could see the water hole. There was a dark mass at the edge of it, where no dark mass should be, and that seemed to be what had disturbed the cattle.

'Something drinking at the water hole,' he reported. 'Could be a man, but if so, he's carrying a bag on his back. And I don't think he'd bother the cattle so much.'

'What else could it be?' she asked.

He chuckled.

'Could be a bear,' he said, and felt her stiffen against his arm. As she did so, the shapeless mass rose from the water and he saw that it was indeed a bear, a big, black bear nearly six feet tall. It sat back on its haunches and snuffed the air, then turned its head, moving its muzzle from side to side, and looked directly up the hill towards them.

The girl gave a little 'yip' of nerves and the bear threw its head back and roared. In the valley it was a menacing noise, and the cattle began to move around nervously.

'Can you shoot him?' she said. 'Or is it better to leave him alone and hope he'll go away?'

'Depends. Bears is notional. Maybe he'll go away by himself now he's had his drink. But he thinks this is his territory and we ain't no right here. In which case, he's more likely to drive us out.'

'Can't you shoot him?'

He took another look through the glasses. The bear sure was big, but he'd yet to come across one that was bullet proof. He told the girl this, without taking his attention from the bear. It seemed undecided, sitting on its haunches and staring up the hill towards them, but eventually it made up its mind, and went off in the opposite direction, rolling like a drunk in a loose-fitting fur coat.

The longhorns watched it go warily but when it had gone out of sight, they gradually relaxed their attention and began to eat grass. For some reason the bear had not actually paid them any attention, which indicated he was not hungry.

Sauermann shook out a loop and roped and saddled his horse. When Horn asked him where he was going, he pointed after the bear.

'I want to see where that varmint went,' he said. 'Bears is notional, and he didn't have a notion to eat beef today. Don't mean he won't have tomorrow. Also, I reckon he'll lie up now he's had his meat and his drink. I want to see where he calls home.'

Horn looked at him dubiously. Bears, as the old man said, were indeed notional. There was nothing to stop this one taking a notion to resent being followed home, and in that case they were likely to lose their stockman.

'I'll come with you,' he said, and reached for his saddle. Sauermann shook his head.

'We can't leave Miz Jemima alone,' he said. 'Them beeves won't be hard to track, if they come through that dust bowl, and if we did it, they can, too. I

118

ain't aiming to take no chances with a bear that size. But I ain't seen no tracks in the home valley, and if there'd been any, I would have.'

'So where does he hang his hat? I think we need to know, and I'm going to find out. I'll feel a mite safer when we do know.'

It made sense, and they had so many of the rustlers' cows that they would be bound to be searching for them by now. Someone needed to stay here to stand guard, and he was the only one who could.

He nodded, but saddled up anyway. He wanted to take a look down the trail towards the valley. Something had been said which had given him an idea, and he wanted to see that trail in daylight, now that it had been travelled by so many cattle.

He left Jemima on guard in the little cave which gave a good field of fire, and a view over the grazing cattle, and turned his horse's head towards the entrance to the valley.

9

He rode out of the valley and on to the horrifying eyebrow trail. The sight of the scratch in the rock up which they had driven all those cattle in full dark made him queasy, but he swallowed hard and followed the trail back down the pass as far as the dust bowl. On the rock there were a few scratches where a hoof had slipped or a pebble had been crushed, but there were certainly no tracks for a pursuer to follow.

The dust bowl was similarly trackless, for the opposite reason. The dust was so fine that it carried no clear imprints of anything.

On the other hand, if just one rustler had seen people moving cattle in the night, it was possible that at least one knew which way they had gone. Horn was sitting his saddle, wondering what to do about it, when he heard voices faintly coming from down the canyon.

There was nowhere for him to hide within easy sight of the canyon except in one of the crevices against the wall of the mountain, and though it might conceal a man on his horse from riders coming up from the dustbowl, they would be bound to see him when they got far enough up the trail.

He had no choice, so he backed the horse into one of the crevices along the trail, and slid the Henry from the saddle boot, which he had adapted to left hand use. As he jacked a cartridge into the breech he heard coughing and spluttering in the dust, and a cloud of it rose and filled the narrow canyon.

Eventually three men emerged through the cloud, coughing and slapping at their clothes and raising their own tiny clouds. They rode out on to the bare rock, and stopped, staring up the eyebrow trail. One of them stepped down and looked at the rock. The others stayed on their horses and looked around.

'You reckon that's a trail?' said one of

the mounted men. 'Looks more like a scratch in the rock to me. If there is a trail, it's got to be down there.' He pointed down into the depths of the canyon.

The dismounted man walked to the edge of the shelf and looked down. The bulge of the rock prevented him seeing into the depths of the canyon, but obviously he wasn't going to risk going down there.

'No way you could get cows down there. You'd have to crank them down with a rope,' he said dismissively. 'Nope, they ain't come this way, no matter what them Target gunnies said. They been driven someplace else and hidden in the night. My guess is you take a deep enough sniff, you'll smell the rebranding fires down in the valley. There's at least three different outfits besides us in there this minute. I vote we go and pay them all a call and take us a look to see what they been branding, and what with.'

He was pulling his bandanna over his

nose and mouth as he said it, turning his horse to go back into the dust bowl, or he might have heard a noise very much like a man clamping his hand over his horse's nostrils because it was about to whinny at the outlaws' horses. As it was the horse got out a kind of strangled mumble, but by that time the rustlers were plunged into the dust cloud and their coughing drowned out any other sound in the canyon.

Horn swung back into the saddle and listened until the sound of coughing men and horses had faded away. Then he turned back and rode up the trail, thinking deeply. If this worked out, they would not need an army to get the outlaws off the Flatbush. Their manpower was already there.

Sauermann was already back from his bear hunt when Horn rode in. The old man looked exhausted again, and for the first time Horn was worried about him. He was so used to the old cowman being made of whipcord that he had forgotten that even whipcord gets stressed and frayed.

'Bear's got a den over at the far end of the valley, in some rocks,' he reported. 'A few miles from here. Didn't see no dead cows on the way, so he's eating something else. Good few deer in the valley over towards the trees at that east end, so maybe he's a weakness for venison.'

'But just here's the only place he can rely on water. I seen a couple of tanks down that way, but one was dry and the other near as dammit — begging your pardon, ma'am — so that's why he was over this way, I reckon. Same token, he'll be back. We'll have to be right careful around here. Don't go away from the cave without a gun, and if you have to use it, keep firing until you're sure he's dead. Don't worry about letting the rustlers know we're here. If that bear gets you, we won't be.'

He drank coffee and chewed on the jerky they had brought with them. His face looked more tightly drawn today than it had the previous day, and Horn refilled his coffee cup.

'Stay there. We need you strong and rested,' he said. 'The work's fallen on you this past few days. You know about cows. You knew the way up here in the dark. You herded, we did what we were told.'

Sauermann's face flushed. 'You saying I ain't fit?' he snapped.

'If you wasn't fit you'd be dead by now. Sure you're fit. Fit as a butcher's dog. There ain't no shame in getting tired, and you're tired now. Lie back and sleep it off. I got an idea for getting them rustlers to do our work for us, and it means we all got to be fit and move fast.'

He rode out round the herd, eye open for bear tracks. There were no new ones, but he did not trust any bear he could not see, and he could not see this one at this moment. He wished he had shot it when it appeared in the first place, but he had no idea whether the searching cowboys were within earshot or not.

Still uneasy, he loped his horse down the valley to within sight of the far end and found it just as Sauermann had said. There was no sign of the bear, and there were several big piles of rock fallen from the walls, so he gave the area a careful survey and was turning away when a movement caught his eye.

It was a mule deer, its ears flapping back and forth like a butterfly's wings, picking a careful path through the rocks near the end of the valley. Behind it came another and little further up the slope, a third. They were walking carefully enough, but then that was in the nature of the animal. But they were definitely not terrified, as he would have expected them to be in an area where there was a hunting bear.

He got out his field glasses and swept the end of the valley. It was craggy, with the usual piles of detritus that had fallen from the walls and piled around their foot. The ponderosas were scattered along and across the end of the valley, clumped here and there, but forming a thin screen. He rode up to a few of the larger trees and looked at the bark. It was untouched and unbroken. Yet he knew that bears marked their hunting territory by leaving deep scratches in the bark of the trees. So where were the marks from this bear?

Pondering what he had seen, he turned his horse back towards the camp, and noted as he rode how the cattle had spread across the floor where there was grass. They were feeding serenely, as though on their home range.

No nervousness about a major predator in their surroundings. Why not?

He rode close to the nearest few and took a closer look at their brands. There were several, most of them simple and therefore simple to brand over. The new-looking brands had been over-branded with either a disc within a circle or the Broken Z he had seen before. Both were easily imposed on other brands.

There were also, however, some

cattle which had not been rebranded: a number of Circle C — easy to turn into Bullseye — and one or two which almost invited the Broken Z.

Easy enough to spot from close up but give them a week or so for the brand to heal and they would be almost impossible to pick out from a herd. The only way to be certain would be to shoot the beast and check the brand from the inside of the hide, where the imposed alteration could be seen.

Pondering, he rode back to the cave and stripped the saddle off his horse. He hobbled the animal and turned it loose to find feed.

Jemima was cleaning. First the cave, then the surroundings, and last of all her own guns. Her pistol, loaded, lay beside her on the rock while she stripped down her Winchester and wiped dust from it. The fine, sandy dust from the canyon had penetrated into the action, and she was cleaning it out with a brush and pull-through. Strangely, her attention to the task made her look more like a woman working in her home than a crack shot dealing with the deadly tools of her trade.

He knelt next to her and wiped his own guns with her oily rag, returning the Colt to the holster when he had finished.

'So. Tell me your idea,' she said, pulling the wad through the rifle barrel with an 'oof' of effort. It came out clean.

'How did you know I have an idea?'

'Sticking out all over you like spines on a cholla. Come on, talk.'

He leaned forward and used the end of his knife to make marks on the ground.

'Far as I can make out, the three or four outfits there at the moment are camped well apart. Hardly surprising when you reckon they's all thieves and thieves never trust anybody.'

'So?'

'So those gunmen I saw down at the pass didn't look real careful for tracks because they thought they already knew where their cows had gone. They were going back to search for them among the other gangs' herds.'

'All the better. They won't come up here, then?'

Well, by his reckoning they probably would in the end if they were allowed to sit down and work it out for themselves. But if they were not, if they were hit while the tempers were already running hot and high, they wouldn't sit down and talk. They would go for their guns.

If they went on losing cows at a rate of a few in a night, tempers would stay high. Rage would overcome reason. It would not be long before, among dishonest men under pressure, somebody could lose his temper.

'How could we make them do that?'

'Take a few cows each night for a few nights, rebrand 'em and filter them back into the valley a few nights later, with raw brands. Sooner or later, one of the gun happy crowd is going to put two and two together and make twenty-five. They'll be stringing each other up from trees sooner than you can count.'

The other two stared at him for a few seconds, open-mouthed. Then Sauermann gave one of his graveyard snorts of laughter.

'You sure as shooting ain't just a pretty face, mister.'

'Or even got one,' said Jemima, with a with a twisted grin. 'But you do seem to know a whole lot more about stealing cows and making trouble than anybody I ever met. I'm glad you were on our side, Luke, I surely am. But we haven't got a branding-iron. How are we going to change the brands?'

He reached into his bedroll and pulled out the running iron he had taken from the rustler.

'With their own iron, ma'am. This one I got from one of the gunnies guarding the herd last night. Seems a pity to waste it.'

★ ★ ★

They started their branding right away with some of the cattle they had stolen the previous night. Horn made a fire and changed the brands on a dozen cows. He changed most of them from an honest Circle C to the rustlers' Bullseye which was simple enough because all he needed to do was close the ends of the C and fill in the centre to make it into a Bullseye. Broken Z was more tricky because it was designed to be. It consisted of two letter Vs arranged on their side to make a Z with a gap in the diagonal. However, he designed a new brand altogether which covered it beautifully: the Double Arrow. By adding a shaft to each of the Vs and a simple feathered flight to the ends of the shaft he had two arrows with hardly a waver. He rather liked it, too.

'Right purty,' drawled Sauermann, watching him from the saddle. 'We could use that one our own selves once we got rid of these lowlife cattle thieves.'

They kept their rebranded two dozen

steers in a roped-off corner of the little valley, and that night they drifted them down the trail. The Broken Z herd was on the nearest pasture to the ranch house, so easing the rebranded cattle in among them was going to be tricky. In any case, they did not want them too well hidden, or they might not be found while their new brands were still raw enough to be obvious.

They drifted the cattle across the open ground as silently as they could, and left them on the near side of the main body of the herd, where any passing cowhand would be bound to notice them. Then they let two of them wander where they would.

They were heading for the pass again when they heard horses being hard-ridden ahead. There was nowhere to hide, so they pulled their horses down on the open ground among some sleeping longhorns and lay across their necks to stop them raising their heads while the riders went by.

The men came on, riding carefully,

until they were in the middle of the herd, then Horn thought he and his companions had been seen. But the riders pulled up by one of the longhorns and, as the beast awakened and started to rise, two of them dropped a loop over its horns to hold it in place and the third caught its hind feet and brought it down again. Then he circled round the prostrate beast and snapped a match on his thumbnail.

For a moment, Horn thought he was lighting a cigarette until the man leaned over the steer and peered at its hip. He gave a grunt of disgust and the match went out.

'What is it?' called one of the other riders and the man on the ground shook his head.

'Circle C. Ain't been rebranded yet,' he answered. 'Maybe we're barking up the wrong tree.'

The other rider shook his head. 'Right tree, wrong cow,' he said savagely. 'I just know that Fletch Brittan's in this somewhere. Ain't trusted him since I seen him palm an ace on me in a poker game back when. He never gives anybody an even break, that polecat. We keep looking, we'll find one sooner or later and when we do I'm going to make him eat it, horns, hide and tail.'

The other rider was too busy recovering his rope and rewinding it to argue, but the set of his shoulders said a whole heap in the moonlight. He didn't agree.

On the other hand, if they could work out which outfit the shady Fletch belonged to, there was a smouldering fire that could be fanned into life. The information was filed away in Luke's mind for later.

But the night had not stopped being interesting. As they were turning away, one of the riders suddenly gave an exclamation, and leaned nearer to a steer which was standing and licking at its own flank.

'Drop a loop on this one,' he said. 'He's got something wrong with his hip and I'll go a dollar I know what it is.'

The steer was roped and a match struck. Exclamations came from all three men.

'Who the hell is Double Arrow?'

'Don't know, but I'll bet Les Black could tell us. Bring that steer along and we'll ask him. He's camped at the ranch house.'

'No,' said one of the his companions. 'He's forted up in the ranch house. We'll wait until he comes out in the morning, and can't hide behind all that wood and stone. Then we'll ask him. Bring the cow along anyhow, and we'll have him to hand. Keep an eye open for any others you see. Where there's one, there'll be more.'

They rode away towards their own camp, towing the steer with them.

Slowly, the Flatbush party got to its feet and remounted.

'It's started,' said Horn. 'We need more branded steers down here. Can you think of anywhere we can put them that will look like a hiding-place badly chosen?'

Sauermann gave one of his dry grunts of laughter.

'Got just the place. Right by the ranch house, too. She'll be right tricky to get them into but once in, they'll be in the perfect place. Let's go brand 'em.'

10

Now that they had decided which outfit to victimize, the work went fast. They turned more and more Broken Z steers into Double Arrow — badly — and filtered them into the temporary corral in the valley. It was in a little dip against the valley wall, which might have looked well-hidden until a rider went on to a little rise nearby, which gave him a perfect overview of the cattle there.

Newly branded cattle, obviously recently and badly branded, made noise and milled around until the brand was healed, and these were no exception. They were restless, and once they had been penned up in their little dip, they became more and more vocal.

Eventually a Broken Z rider passed close enough to wonder what cattle were making such a fuss, and went to have a look. What he found, unsurprisingly, sent him lickety-split for Lester Black at the ranch house. They came back with a third man.

It was the third man who bothered Horn most because he was wearing buckskins and had a feather in his hat. He looked like a tracker, and as soon as he got to the temporary corral he dropped off his horse and went on one knee.

So he was in fact a tracker. Bad news. He would find horse tracks among the cattle prints, and he would recognize them again as he went about the basin.

Horn was keeping watch from a small outcropping halfway along the wall of the valley, where there was enough hidden space to put his horse, and enough height to look down into their improvised corral.

He ran events back in his mind and realized that if there were any prints there for the tracker to read, they would be his, Horn's prints. He had faded a few more rebranded cattle into the valley in the early hours of the morning, guiding them gently and letting them make their own way to the corral. He had water and food for the day, and he was expecting the other two to bring down more steers in the night.

The tracker put paid to those plans. While keeping a wary eye on him, Horn began to ready himself to leave his vantage point and make for the far side of the valley. If possible he must keep the tracker from the hidden canyon which led through the dust bowl to the mountain trail.

But events were going faster than he had expected. While the tracker was still leaning over the hoofprints in the ground, a couple of men appeared, leading a haltered steer. The steer was a big one, and did not like being led, so it was giving them trouble. They would have done better to drive it, Horn thought, and grinned wryly as he realized he was awakening his old cattle knowledge by his activities now.

The two men and their steer arrived

at the Black party while the tracker was still trying to read the tracks, and they messed up the ground. Horn could tell that from the quick, irritable movements of the tracker when he stood up, and one of the riders reacted angrily. Words were exchanged, and the Indian climbed back on to his horse and turned away, angrily. Black called after him but the man did not look back, and cantered off in the direction of the ranch house.

The arrival of the two men leading the steer was not a happy event. The brand was pointed at, examined, knowledge of it was denied and the denial disbelieved. The newcomers rode off with their steer, and Horn wondered what they were going to do with it.

Whatever they decided, the seeds of suspicion were obviously sprouting into blooms, which was what he wanted. He leaned back against his rock and rolled himself a couple of coffin-nail cigarettes, laying them on the rock to wait until possible observers were gone.

The morning passed quickly. More riders were summoned from the ranch house, and collected the rebranded cattle, taking them down to the ranch. The various other animals he had seeded around the valley would turn up sooner or later and the suspicions would mount.

To the other rustlers, it would look as though the Broken Z outfit was establishing its own extra brand, into which their cows could be added. To the Broken Z boys, it looked as though somebody else was stealing Broken Z cows and rebranding them.

Since Broken Z was the biggest team in the valley, had in fact set up the rustling hideaway, it looked as though they were establishing a new herd. Why would they do that if not to steal the other rustlers' cattle?

That suited Horn just fine, and he settled down to doze away the morning in the shade, with one eye half-open in case the tracker should reappear. In the heat of the day, his horse, relieved to be in the shade, cropped the grass in the little corner and snoozed with its head down and one hoof lifted.

★ ★ ★

The first signs of trouble came in the early evening when Horn heard shots snapping away from the eastern end of the valley where the Bullseye outfit had made their camp. He awakened from his half-doze and focused his field glasses over there, but he was too far away and heat haze was too thick for him to see anything.

In any case, he asked himself, why Bullseye? They were doing their own rebranding, presumably of stolen Circle C stock, and were not involved in his plans, yet.

He was just making up his mind to go over there and see what was going on when he noticed that the tracker was back, and was examining the ground where the cattle had been held, with interest. If he was any use it would not take him long to realize that there were some unfamiliar tracks in there and start wondering whose they were.

Since his arm injury, now mostly healed, he had been shooting from his left shoulder and with his left hand. He was competent with both and, when pushed could handle his rifle from the right shoulder. But he was no longer a fast draw. His right hand would hold the Colt, but his previous panther speed with it had gone, and he suspected it had gone for good. Give him time and he was still a good shot. But his days as a fast draw gunman were over.

He was not upset about it. The profession of gunman had never attracted him. It was simply the only thing he could do after the war was over, and he had dropped into it almost by accident. A rancher was being squeezed by a rustler, and his hands were valiant but not warriors.

The rancher had offered what sounded like a fat fee for protection for his herd, and Horn was broke. He took the job and he was lucky. He ran down the rustlers on the first morning on the job, while they were branding their stolen steers, and rode up to their camp.

'Branding?' he said mildly, and met an ugly reception.

'What is it to you?' growled the man with the running iron, while his two companions started to sidle off to the sides.

'They move any further, and I'll kill you first and them next,' Horn told him.

He was young and gangling, and he was still wearing his Union blue pants as breeches. Above all, he did not look dangerous.

The man threw the branding-iron at him and went for his gun. Horn shot the other two and then the brander. All three shots were spot-on target, which was noted by the sheriff when Horn brought them in, hanging face down over their saddles. The townsfolk looked thoughtfully at the cadavers and even more thoughtfully at the gangling young man and drew their own conclusions.

'Horn?' said the town sage. 'Ain't I heard of you before? Up from Texas?'

He denied it because it was not true but they didn't believe him. In the end he gave up trying to convince them and let it ride. His real origins were no worse than Texas and no better, and he got tired of arguments which always threatened to turn into a fight.

Now he needed the speed, but he had not got it, so he was training himself to be a sure shot rather than a fast one. It remained to be seen whether it would work as well, but after all, what choice had he?

He watched the tracker narrowly. The man was on his own this time and Horn wondered whether he had come back of his own accord or had been sent. Not that it made much difference.

He drew a bead on the bending man reluctantly. The tracker was, after all, doing his job, which was all he was supposed to do. It was bad luck he was doing it for the opposite side.

There was another popping of guns

from across the valley, and once again Horn could not see who was shooting at whom. The effect on the tracker, though, was galvanic.

He ran for his horse, threw himself into the saddle and sent his horse racing for the other side of the valley.

Now that he was unwatched for a while, Horn took his chance to make off. He threw his traps into his saddle-bags, tightened the cinches and climbed on to the horse, which was glad of some exercise.

Now that he knew there was an Indian tracker around, Horn took more care with his movements. He followed the trail down which they had brought the rebranded steers, and took the occasional side-swing through rougher ground to confuse his tracks.

As a result of which he took longer than he had intended, and found himself making for the hidden canyon in swiftly gathering dusk.

By pure chance he glanced back down into the valley as he was about to swing behind the great rock which marked the entrance, and saw out of the corner of his eye a faint flicker of movement along his back trail.

There were loose steers wandering on the valley floor, and the small night creatures were beginning to came out in the dusk, but this looked to be too large a movement for either. He halted the horse behind the rock and stared off to the side of where he thought he'd seen the movement. Looking directly at things in the dusk often had the reverse of the desired effect, he found. He had heard a wandering medicine showman with more than the usual knowledge refer to it as 'peripheral vision', but whatever the long-winded term, it boiled down to looking near the target, not at it. And it worked fine.

He saw the movement repeated and after staring for a while saw it turn into a man on a horse, coming along carefully, and taking care not to catch up.

So he had not managed to throw off

the tracker. He cursed to himself, but it was too late now to try and avoid the man again. He must have seen Horn disappear behind the rock, and a reappearance would be too obvious.

Horn dropped off the horse and ground-hitched him, then ran round the back of the rock and took a look out from the other side. From this side, and looking as he was towards the west, he could see the rider approaching cautiously. He was leaning from the saddle from time to time to check the ground, but very soon it would be too dark to see the tracks, and as Horn watched him he straightened up suddenly and stared direct at Horn's hiding place.

For a moment the two men stared at one another in the dusk, then the tracker dropped down across his horse's withers and the animal whirled away, going from its careful walk to a flat run in an instant. With its rider a mere lump on the animal's back, travelling fast away from him, the chance of a hit was small, and the noise of the shot would likely bring other riders.

Horn put up his rifle, watched until the rider was out of sight and walked back to his horse. It greeted him with a shake of the head.

'Yeah, I know. I should have seen him back when. He followed me a while across the basin,' he told it, and hoisted himself into the saddle.

The trouble was that the man would be coming back in the morning with a a party of riders. He had no idea whether he had been seen waiting in ambush or if the tracker was one of those men with an instinctive feel for danger, who had sensed it and taken the wisest course of getting away without taking a risk.

It did not really make any difference. The damage was done. He needed to warn the others.

He rode through the dust bowl with his bandanna held over his nostrils, and cautiously up the eyebrow trail beyond. For the first time, he was really worried.

11

He met Sauermann and the girl at the top of the trail, just about to start feeding twenty steers down to the valley and stopped them to explain. Together they went back to their campsite and he began to pack his traps into the saddle-bags. They did the same.

'Kind of embarrassing,' he admitted. 'We haven't seen this guy before, and I didn't know he was in the valley. Don't rightly see why he is, but he's there, and he knows about me, if all's what it looks like. He also knows about the canyon behind the rock.'

Sauermann busied himself building a fire, and stuck the coffee pot into the side where it would warm up.

'Your horse needs a rest if you been trailing all over the valley all day,' he said as he worked. 'Pass me that skillet, will you? You need to eat and if we're going on the run, we'd all better have something.'

Without asking the girl had gone down the slope to a place where she could keep an eye on the valley entrance. By now the moon was coming up and the floor of the place was brightly lit in silver and shadowed in deep black. The meat hissed in the skillet and Horn could smell the coffee from the fire. He had to keep swallowing to avoid dribbling.

'Didn't know I was so hungry,' he muttered, when Sauermann handed him a plate with campfire bread and a hunk of steaming meat on the side. He had found some wild onions some-where, and the fragrance filled the cave.

'Don't talk. Eat,' said Jemima, coming back to the fire while Sauer-mann took his plate out to the lookout point, juggling with a cup of hot coffee on the way. Jemima sat next to Horn and crammed meat in her mouth. Horn did as he was told, and the cave was silent for a while.

'What do we do now?' she said when there was enough room in her mouth for words as well as food. 'Will they come up here, you think?'

He nodded in the firelight. They had to, now that he had been seen. They would not know who he was, of course. Only a couple of them had actually ever seen him in daylight and so far as the invaders of the valley knew, he had disappeared after being shot. The girl and Sauermann had disappeared at the same time, and the outlaws had no reason to suppose they were still around.

What he was worried about was that one of the rustlers might put two and two together and make an all too accurate four. If they realized that the cattle movements and the rebranding was being done by outsiders, his scheme for putting them at one another's throats was a non-starter.

'But suppose they don't?' she said suddenly. 'That tracker has only seen you from behind in the dusk. He can't know you aren't anything to do with one of the outfits in the valley.'

Well, he might, because a tracker read hoof prints, and given time he would realize the prints from Horn's mustang were not among the regular traffic in the valley. But that would take him time, and when he had done it, he still might not draw the conclusion that there was a new bunch interfering.

But this would all be beside the point once the tracker came up that eyebrow trail and found the rebranded cattle in the valley. A half-dozen men could sweep the place from end to end, and to them it would not matter whom they caught, so long as they caught someone.

He wiped his plate with a handful of grass and poured more coffee, then took the pot out to Sauermann for a refill. The old man was propped between two rocks, his back against one and his feet against another, with his Winchester across his knees, and he accepted the drink gladly.

'What do you reckon?' he asked. Horn dropped to his haunches beside him.

'That tracker's either an Indian or a half-breed. He was in buckskins and he had a feather in his hat,' he said, considering. No white man would wear a feather in this region, where it had so often been an invitation to shoot.

'Or he could just live with Indians, maybe have an Indian wife,' said the old cowpuncher. 'Some do.'

Horn glanced at him. 'You ever do it?'

Sauermann nodded. 'Spent four winters with the Mescaleros, back a bit,' he said. 'Had me an Apache wife and a little boy, back then. Bright little feller, he was, and she was purtier than a three-week calf. Hard folk, but they was family. Means a lot to them, family. Meant a lot to me, too.'

Horn glanced at him, surprised. 'Why didn't you stay?'

The old man shrugged. 'Mexicans. Scalp-hunters, likely, or maybe slavers, but up from south of the border anyways. They attacked the village, and we fought them off. Killed a few and the rest ran. But they did some damage while they was there. Killed my family. That's how I knew what you was feeling.'

Horn hung his head. The story was repeated time and again in the Territory. The bitterness inflicted by each side on the other would never wear off, he thought, but he did not want to inflict deeper hurt.

The old man shifted in his seat. He was rolling a cigarette and ducked his head behind his hat while he lit it and kept the burning end within his hand. From ten feet away it would be invisible, Horn knew.

'Must make a man bitter, that,' he ventured. The old man shrugged a movement more felt than seen in the moonlight.

'Not bitter, no,' he said quietly. 'Made me mad at the time, though. I followed the survivors of that group all the way down into the borders. Four of them, there was when I started.'

'You catch them?'

The old man gave one of his dry coughing laughs. 'Oh, yeah. Took me a while. They split up. But I caught them all in the end. Nobody takes the hair offen my family and rides home with it.'

'You killed them all?'

'In the end they was all dead. Took them a while.'

He had spent years with the Apaches. Horn thought briefly on why it had taken the scalp hunters a while to die, and swallowed hard, several times. He needed to.

The old man stiffened suddenly and peered down into the valley. Horn tried to follow his pointing hand but could see nothing but the shifting patterns of the moonlight and the sleeping cattle.

Then he noticed what had caught Sauermann's attention. Over towards the seep the cattle were beginning to move. One stood up suddenly and lifted its head, then another did the same

157

thing. Their heads were turned in the same direction and they began to move uneasily.

'That damned tracker made it up here after all,' Horn growled. But the old man shook his head.

'He'd come in from the canyon end,' he said. 'They're looking the other way. I reckon it's that darned bear back for his supper. I should have dropped that critter when I got him in my sights.'

In the dark it was impossible to make out any details, and Horn could not see any sign of the bear who was presumably just another of the dark shadows down there. But the way the cows were moving gave some indication of where it was.

He stood up, reached back into the cave and pulled the Henry towards him, working the lever as he did so. A dull pang in his right shoulder reminded him to put it to his left.

'Can you see him?' The old man had his own rifle ready, but Horn shook his head.

'I know he's down there, because of the cows. But just where, I don't know.'

The strange thing was that he did know where the animal was. Every steer he could see was now standing up and all their heads pointed the same way. The bear was where they were looking, and he could see nothing there at all. The bear was there, the bear was moving, and from the nervous way the cattle were beginning to mill about, the bear was hunting.

Every now and again he thought he had it, when he could swear he had seen one of the patches of deeper shadow make a movement, but it always turned out to be his eyes which were finding what they expected, and not what was there.

'Watch the cows,' murmured Sauermann. 'Look where they're looking.'

Horn stared at them. Their heads had moved since he last looked and they seemed to be looking in his direction. Perhaps, he thought vaguely, they were able to hear the two men talking.

Sauermann was quicker off the mark than he. Suddenly he swore loudly and shouted: 'Jemima! Watch out!'

At the same moment, Horn caught a whiff so foul and redolent of rotting meat that it almost made him gag. He threw himself backwards and out of the gap between the rocks just as there was a snuffling roar and a shapeless mass of fur and fury came over the far side and fell into it.

Sauermann was on his feet on top of one of the rocks, and his Winchester was banging away like a whole regiment of riflemen, the flashes lighting the little hollow between the rocks in which they had just been sitting.

The night was full of roars and the moonlight magnified the bear to impossible proportions, a mass of black in which the moonlight caught the glint of teeth and claws. Horn was working the lever of his Henry as fast as his mending arm would go, pumping lead into the black, roaring mass.

Something that felt like a steam

locomotive hit him in the stomach and fired him backwards out of the little hollow to hit the stony slope several yards away. As he went, his rifle discharged itself.

And then, suddenly, it was over.

He rolled over and found himself still trying to kill the bear. He was sitting on one leg, the other extended in front of him, and his right arm was trying to work the loading lever of his now empty rifle.

★　★　★

The bear was dead. The following morning in the light they counted fifteen bullets in it, any of which would have killed it in the end. Which one had actually done the job it was difficult to work out, and they wrangled amiably over it all day.

When they counted up, they had fired twenty-five shots, which meant that ten had missed altogether at ranges of up to six feet. It was a miracle they had not, in that tiny space, shot one another, but Horn was the only one to have been touched, and they watched through the following day as his stomach turned into one huge bruise. It was painful, but the most sympathy he got was a grunt of amusement from Sauermann. The old man worked one of his medical miracles, though, by producing a smelly poultice from some herbs growing down near the seep, which he slapped on the blue-black stomach. Like almost all of Sauermann's rough and ready medicines it smelled, but also like all of them, it worked. The pain eased after a couple of hours, and Horn was able to climb on to his horse and help round up the steers in the little valley.

Since the bear was no longer down at the far end to keep them away, they hazed the cattle down that way. There was grass down there which had not been cropped yet, and the steers went readily enough, and as though to give them time to clear out, the tracker and the expected search party did not turn up.

By mid afternoon, they had moved their camp down to the end of the valley, where they found the bear's cave simply by sniffing. It stank of bear and long dead meat.

'But I'd have expected worse,' said Sauermann, hooking his knee over his saddle horn and rolling one of his coffin nails. 'Generally, bears bury their kills when they reckon they've eaten enough, and you can find them just by following the wind.'

Horn, who reckoned he could have found this one from Kentucky with the wind in the right direction, gave him an old-fashioned look and rubbed his stomach.

'Leave it alone,' Jemima told him sharply. 'You'll just rub it sore again.' Since she was right and it was becoming sore, he obeyed.

They made their camp in one of the other caves, where their fire could not be seen from outside. Sauermann produced more of his foul smelling weeds and laid them on Horn's stomach with surprising gentleness.

'You get some sleep,' he said. 'We'll wake you towards dawn. Going to be one hell of a busy day tomorrow.'

He was right, too. In the morning, the tracker found them.

12

He came like the bear, silent and almost invisible. And like the bear, it was the cattle who gave him away. Jemima was on watch at the time, and she noticed first one and then another head come up and point up the valley to the entrance.

She reached behind her and prodded Sauermann with the end of her rifle barrel. He sat up, instantly awake, and roused Luke Horn in turn. They spread out along the foot of the cliff and stared south as one and then another of the steers raised its head and looked.

As they had with the bear, the steers indicated the tracker simply by looking where he was. He had taken a route along the north side of the little valley, tucking himself into the steep rock wall there, and inching his way down.

There was no real need for him to

track them. He must have followed Horn's hoofprints to the canyon, and steeled himself to the eyebrow trail. All he had to do was follow the cattle droppings higher up and they had led him to the valley entrance. Inside it were the traces of grazing cattle round the seep.

He had found the body of the bear, and counted the bullets it had taken to kill it with interest. He gave a grunt of deep respect over the corpse and made a mental note to come back and claim the pelt when he had finished with today's business. Then he had pushed on along the valley, staying off the tracks because he could see them clearly enough from a distance, and he did not want to mix them with his own.

By now he knew there were three riders, one of them significantly lighter than the other two, which gave him grounds for hoping it was a woman. The same discovery delayed his decision to ride back and raise a search party. He did not want to share her with anybody else, or at any rate, not yet.

The thought of the woman distracted him at a time when he needed to use all his concentration. He could not push the hot thoughts of her out of his mind, and when he should have been thinking about what awaited him when he got to the end of the trail, he was already thinking about the possibilities of the next few hours with her.

But he was not tracking a woman. He was tracking three tough fugitives, of which she was by no means less dangerous than either of the others. Horn was a man long trained in the art of staying alive while being in himself a killer. Fed Sauermann had fought in several wars, including the War Between the States. Jemima Penrose was a crack shot who had been harried out of her home and land and was very, very deep-down angry about it.

The tracker, who was known to all who rode the outlaw trail and distrusted by most, went by the name of

Injun Jim. He sidled along the side of the canyon, dropping into the various side canyons on his way, until he had reached the end where logically his quarry had to be.

He was aware that the cattle were giving his presence away, but he also knew that nobody knew exactly where he was — merely that he was somewhere along the wall to the north.

It was pure chance that he came across Jemima first. He had to admit she had picked herself a good place, a little away from the canyon wall, between two rocks and looking back the way he had come. She had missed seeing him because he had dismounted and she was expecting a mounted man.

She was prettier than he had expected, which was a bonus for him and excited him greatly. He reached out with his rifle barrel and prodded her foot. She rolled over and looked straight at him.

'Don't shoot', she said quietly. 'It will warn the others.'

'Ain't no others, missy. Just you and me.' He grinned, not quite understanding why she did not want 'the others' alerted, but by this time his mind was filled with disturbing pictures, and he did not bother to withdraw and work it out.

It was not until the hand clamped on to his forehead and forced his head back, the weight of the man behind him bore him to the ground and the burning pain of the knife slitting his throat filled his mouth with blood and choked his dying moan that he realized she had not been talking to him.

★   ★   ★

'If that there was the truth, we got more time than we thought,' said Sauermann, wiping his knife on the dead man's buckskin shirt fastidiously. Horn was surprised but not shocked by the expert, silent, killing. He knew the old man had lived with the Apache, but he had not bothered to follow his thinking through to its logical end.

It did not occur to him until later that for a sniper, whose business was murder from a distance, being finicky about the expertise of another killer was ridiculous.

For the moment, though, he followed the line of the canyon wall back until he found the tracker's horse, ground-hitched in an alcove. He led it back to their own stock, where it joined in the cropping of the sparse grass without causing a ripple.

'If he could find us so could anybody else,' said Jemima. 'I thought we had covered up our tracks.'

'For night tracking, sure. But cows take in grass at one end and let it out the other, and there ain't no stopping them. They leave their own trail and he followed it. Surprised he couldn't smell his way here in the dark. Some of my in-laws could,' said Sauermann. 'One way or other, they'll find the trail and it leads straight here. We got to go.'

She nodded. Common sense said

that once behind the spike of rock that guarded the entrance to the eyebrow trail, any competent tracker would come here. Only the rustlers' own suspicions that one of the other groups in the valley was causing the problem had prevented the first group from finding them days ago.

'What shall we do, then? Try running all the cattle through the canyon and out into the country?' Even as she said it, she realized how ridiculous it was. The rustlers were on their guard now. Any movement would be picked up instantly and bring men with guns after them.

But Horn looked up from packing his bedroll and stared at her.

'That idea's just simple enough to work,' he said slowly. 'Them bad actors is wound up tight enough to explode, right now. Their tracker's gone missing, their cows are being rebranded, more stock is going every other night. They're about ready to explode right now. Maybe now's the time to light the fuse.'

'When?'

'What's wrong with now? We got some rebranded stock here, and some with their original brands. We've even got a dozen or so that they've rebranded theirselves.'

'Tonight, we run them down the canyon and into the valley. Start them going just before dawn and run them right through the nearest herd. We probably couldn't control them once a big lot start going, but so long as they're running, who cares a wet red cent? Running cows got to get out somewhere, and if we just keep them going they'll likely pick up some of the others as they go.'

'You know what a stampede's like. They'll run until they're tuckered out, then they'll stop. By that time they'll be spread out over the countryside like molasses on a hot stone. Take days to get them all gathered up again, and by that time, every cowman within a hundred miles'll be coming to see all that beef, some with half-healed brands, some with the originals, some Broken Z, some Bull-seye — and a good many with Circle C, which is the same thing but ain't healed recent.'

The others stared at him, and smiles broke out on two faces.

'You,' said Jemima, 'are not just a purdy face.'

'He ain't even a purdy face,' growled Sauermann. 'But I have to admit that right now he looks like a right clever one. Saddle up. It'll take the rest of the day to get these beeves a-rolling, and we should have them down at the dust bowl just before dawn.'

★ ★ ★

He was right. The first light from the east found them slapping the dust from their shoulders and coughing it out of their lungs, with the small herd filing through the narrow gap between the sentinel rock and the canyon side. They had made the drive at a slow pace because they wanted the cows to have plenty of energy to run, and in any case trying to hurry them down that hair-raising hump of rock in the dark would have been suicidal.

The cows seemed to feel the same way, for they crowded to the side of the trail against the cliff face and moved cautiously in the dark. One or two of the more cantankerous ones tried to turn back to the valley where they had water and grass, but a heavy coil of rope slapped across their noses changed their ideas and they got to the bottom of the canyon.

By the time they hit the dust bowl they were going confidently enough and the closing walls of the final stretch kept them on track. Their drivers slapped them through the choking clouds with coiled lariats, and in the rosy light of dawn, they poured out of the canyon, round the marker rock and into the valley.

There was a startled shout as they emerged, and the sound of a shot. Then the cattle were out and running and the three who had brought them there came cautiously after them, to find that they had run clear over a campsite which had been set up in the gap between the rock and the wall of the valley.

The cattle flattened the campsite and swept on through. One of the rustlers was caught in his blankets and trampled to death. The other was already mounted and able to run with the cows, though he was a badly frightened man, and never really got over the sight of what he later described as 'a thousand head of maddened beef' coming apparently out of solid rock. Obviously, the original party of rustlers who had discovered the hidden pass had not passed on the information.

The rustlers had penned their stolen stock up against the side of the valley, and when the running cattle exploded in among them they all took off in one panic-stricken body. A solid, fast-moving phalanx of tossing horns and bellowing heads, they swept all before them.

The startled drover who had survived the charge was too busy staying on his horse and out of the way of the hammering hoofs to do much more than head for the higher ground and let the stampede go past him. In the morning light, he could see the cattle, all of them coated with dust so they looked like their own ghosts, with the stock he was supposed to be guarding mixed in among them. He thought he saw equally grey, faceless riders among them, too, but when he told the tale later he was greeted with such jeering incredulity that he left them out of the later versions.

The stampede was even more effective than Horn had hoped. The outlaw herd, half of them branded, was being held between the secret canyon and the natural entrance to the valley. The running animals, by good luck, happened to be able to see the gap in the cliffs which held the entrance to the valley, and perhaps because of that, or because the land dropped away there and they were able to run downhill, or just because of pure dumb luck, that was the way they ran.

Also on that side of the valley was another outfit which was in the middle of branding its stolen cows, and the running cattle's hammering hoofs and frightened bellows sent that herd into a panic as well.

Normally, the running cattle might not have actually kept up their stampede progress to the pass, but panic fed panic. The speed, the hammering hoofs, the bellowing throats and the tossing horns lit a fuse somewhere in the other cattle and they exploded into action.

On the way, they ran through the horse line established by the rustlers, and the saddle horses waiting to be used joined in the running mass. Horns gored them and they screamed like women, which fed the panic.

'Whoo-wee!' said Sauermann when he joined Horn and the girl to one side.

'I never seen cows run like that. Not in all my years with cows, I never. They like to have flown out of that valley.'

'They may yet,' agreed Jemima, who was swabbing dust and perspiration off her face with a bandanna which looked as though it had been used to clean a stable.

Horn was less impressed. Once the panic left them the running cows would simply slow down and stop. If they were outside the valley, they might be well spread out as he had planned, but if they were still within its boundaries, it would be a simple enough job to round them up again.

13

It was not hard to get a firefight going between the rustlers whose cows were currently heading for the desert like a cavalry charge. Even in the valley they raised a cloud of dust which must have been visible for miles out on the desert below, and the two outfits whose stolen steers were currently on the run were constantly popping out of the cloud, shooting their pistols in the air in a vain attempt to head them off.

Both outfits had their bandannas pulled up over their faces to keep out the dust and there was no hope of recognizing people by their clothing. For one thing, the rustlers had been pulled out of their blankets without time to do more than stamp on their boots and grab their hats and guns. For another, the members of one gang did not know the members of the other well enough to recognize them in the dust.

One man had not even taken time to saddle his horse, a fatal mistake since in the roaring madness of the stampede he was quickly knocked from his horse and vanished under several hundred tons of racing beef.

Horn saw him go and winced inwardly at his fate, but Sauermann, who was riding near by, simply shouted: 'One less!' and went on past like a racing rider.

He saw a rider reining in and looking in his direction suspiciously. Horn dropped him with a one-handed shot from the Henry. Then he put the rifle back into the saddle boot and used his Colt to hurry things along.

The danger was that he might fire at Sauermann, who was just another dusty figure in the turmoil, so he made a note of the direction the old man was taking, and went in the opposite one. Congratulating himself on thinking things through, he was nearly shot down by Jemima, who came barrelling through, shrieking like a wounded wildcat and twice as dangerous.

The cattle were slowing. He could see first single animals and then small groups beginning to break way from the main body. They were the ones they had brought down from the high canyon, simply too exhausted to run any further.

They were still within the valley, but he could see as he topped a small hillock that a good number of later additions were still going through the valley entrance and spreading down the hills into the plain beyond.

They were not going as fast, though, and the dust was settling. Time to go. He swung the horse away from the cattle after shooting in the air a couple of times to keep the ones nearest to him moving. Whether it worked or not he could not tell.

He saw a slim cowboy so covered in dust that he might have been a statue, and swung close enough to holler: 'Enough. Ride!'

Jemima waved her pistol at him and pulled her tired horse around heading for the far side of the valley. A stick-thin dust statue emerged from the moving column of cattle and followed her. Horn made sure they were not followed before he made off in turn.

He was surprised that they had not been identified but realized that most of the rustlers did not know of their existence, and many were already inclined to distrust their colleagues. The stampede had merely served to confirm their suspicions.

★ ★ ★

Tired after nearly twenty-four hours' hard work and hard riding, he was slow to react when a rider came out of a stand of junipers ahead of him, wearing a nasty grin. It was Lester Black, and unlike the men who were even now trying to stop the column of cattle leaving the valley, he was not covered in dust. Neither was his Winchester, which was pointed directly at Horn's head.

'I thought one of them riders was kinda light in the saddle,' he said slowly. 'Took me a while to remember you got that damned girl out from under us. It's you been causing me all this trouble this last couple of weeks, ain't it? You got all them owl hoots falling over their own shadows and shooting at each other.'

Horn leaned forward and put his left elbow on the saddle horn. He let his right hand, which was hanging loose at his side, dangle so that each movement made it shake like a curtain in the wind. He saw Black notice it and grin.

'I heard about you, Horn. Killer in the war, killer in the peace. I thought that made you the right man for this job. Guerrillas got no conscience, they say.'

'Can't afford one,' Horn told him easily. 'Get nothing for a conscience, but you'd be right surprised what some of these dirt farmers got buried under their hearths.'

Black's mouth twisted. It was an ugly sight, and the laugh he produced was uglier.

'So what made you break your contract with us? We thought we'd got the right man for the job.'

Horn laughed in his face.

'You made me change my mind. You lied to me. You never told me about the girl. You never told me about the old man you murdered. I don't like liars. I don't like men who prey on women. Above all else, I can't abide a coward.'

For some reason, the last word got to Black. The mocking grin fell from his face, and the rifle quivered in his grasp.

'You'll pay for that crack, mister.'

He brought the rifle to his shoulder.

'Here it comes, killer. You already got one crippled wing. Now here's another.'

He was enjoying himself, so he took his time aiming and cocking the Winchester. While he was taking aim, Horn pulled the Colt from behind his belt buckle with his left hand and shot him through the body.

A Colt .44 will shoot through three inches of pine, and its effect on a human body was much the same. The impact of the big, slow slug must have hit a bone somewhere, for it knocked Black sideways on the horse and he lost his rifle. The blood ran down from the bullet wound spreading over the front of his shirt.

He looked down at it, and raised his head to stare at Horn. Both of them had seen men gut-shot. Black knew he was a dying man and that when the shock wore off he would be a man in agony as well.

'But you lost your fast draw,' he protested, as though Horn had broken some kind of rule of combat. 'You shouldn't be able to draw fast any more.'

Horn held his aim steadily, Black might be going to die — certainly was going to die — but he was not dead yet, and he had nothing to lose.

Still, he was not going to do the dying man any favours.

'I didn't need a fast draw for you,' he said easily. 'You're a talker. You can't just shoot, you got to talk about it first, enjoy it. You like hurting folks. I heard a whole heap of things about you, back down the line, and weren't none of them pretty.'

The shock was beginning to wear off. He saw Black's face twist with the first onset of pain. The man's clutching hand which was clamped over the bullet hole began to slip away from his belly, as though the strength was going out of it.

'Come . . . come closer,' the wounded man moaned. Horn stayed where he was his Colt cocked and unwavering. The dying man heard the double click and his face turned into an animal snarl.

Horn was expecting a trick, but all the man did was drop his hand down by his side. It was the sudden look of triumph that alerted Horn.

He fired once, and then again. Heard the bullets hit home even through hearing dulled by the explosions. Saw the blood fly from Black's right shoulder and then from his head. Saw the now dead man fall from his horse as though his strings had been cut. He was just in time to grab hold of the animal's bridle before it could run.

'There was no need for that!' Jemima's voice was strained and furious. He looked over his shoulder to see that she and Sauermann had turned back and were riding up behind him. They had arrived just in time to see him fire the final shots.

'There was if I want to live,' he said. 'Dying men can kill easy as them with bright futures.'

'Don't try and justify it. I saw you deliberately shoot him twice. He wasn't even reaching for his gun.'

Normally Horn would just have ridden off and let her think what she wanted, but this time he found to his surprise that it really mattered to him that she should not think him a callous killer.

'Sauermann, you mind doing me a favour?'

The old man gave a grunt which he took as assent.

'Get down and look in his right sleeve. The one as was hanging down straight.'

The old man rode over to the dead outlaw and dismounted, hunkered down and began to search him. As he raised the right arm, he gave a surprised grunt, and straightened up, holding a little pistol in his hand. He made to hand it to Horn but the man waved it away.

'Give it to Miz Penrose, will you? I want her to see it straight from you. Treat it like a black widow, though, ma'am. It will be cocked and I'll lay a gold piece to a slice of flapjack it's got a hair trigger.'

The old man carefully uncocked the little sleeve gun before handing it over to his boss. She handled it gingerly.

'Is this a deringer? I've heard of them, but I haven't seen one close up before,' she said, staring down at it. 'Where was it?'

'In his hand,' said Sauermann. 'How did you know?' he asked Horn.

'He gave himself away. He was gut-shot and the pain just started. But he took his hand away from his belly and dropped it to his side. Only way to get the gun into his hand. There'll be a harness up his sleeve. And there was one other thing.'

'What?' she asked.

He smiled. 'Only gut-shot man I ever seen managed to find it funny.'

Sauermann returned to the body and searched through the pockets. He came up with a collection of items so ordinary they almost made the man look harmless. A Barlow knife, bag of tobacco and papers, a small poke of coins, matches, and a wad of printed papers.

'You want these?' he asked Horn, but Horn waved them away. Then: 'Whoa — give me a look at them papers, Fed. May be something there we need to know.'

Sauermann handed them over, but before Horn had a chance to look at them the girl said: 'Riders coming.'

189

They were far away as yet, but definitely coming this way, and they were in a hurry. Horn tucked the papers carefully into the front of his shirt, and they rode away. The last thing Horn wanted was a showdown now, outnumbered and outgunned.

They spurred their tired horses and headed for the hidden canyon, leaving the approaching riders to find the body and draw their own conclusions. There was a startled shout from behind as they went but nobody fired after them and there was no pursuit.

14

The firing broke out as they were approaching the pillar which obscured the canyon entrance. For a moment, they thought they were the target and all of them whirled their horses for a retreat, but the firing went on, and no bullets buzzed about their startled ears.

Horn pulled his horse to a standstill. The firing was close and intense. He had heard the same kind of thing during the war, when two groups of scouts ran into one another unexpectedly. For some reason, the shock of the encounter made the fighting more bitter and intense.

'It's coming from the canyon,' Jemima said suddenly, and he realized that the odd note in the firing was because he was not hearing it direct. It must be echoing inside the canyon, in the dust bowl.

'Stay here,' he said and dismounted, handing the reins to Sauermann. 'If I don't get back, get her out of here and over to the hideout we used first. I'll come for you there.'

Sauermann opened his mouth to protest, took a long look at the set of Horn's face, and nodded tersely.

'Just don't let her down,' he said. 'She sets store by you. You come back, you hear?'

Horn nodded, pulled his Henry from the saddle boot, and ran up the slope to get behind the standing stone and into the canyon mouth. He chose the side away from the trail.

As he had expected, the firing sounded more clearly here. A barrage of shots, then a few isolated ones, followed by another volley.

He climbed to the side of the standing stone, lay flat and took off his hat before peering round the base.

In front of him, half a dozen men were lying or kneeling in a firing line, aiming shots into the cloud of dust in the neck of the canyon. Down there, in the dust, shapes of men on horseback appeared and disappeared as the dust swirled and eddied. They were, like anybody who used the canyon, like moving statues on stone-coloured horses. And they returned a vigorous fire, riding to the mouth of the canyon, blasting away and then disappearing back into the dust.

While he watched the men outside the cloud picked off first one and then another of them. All the men on the outside had to do was keep their volley aimed at the canyon neck where the dust was thinnest, and fire as soon as a shape appeared. They could hardly miss, and they were merciless.

But the dust helped the mounted men as well. They appeared as though from a door, one moment invisible, the next a living, shooting shape. Two of the men waiting in the sniper line had been hit, and lay still, and while he watched a third dropped his Winchester and writhed away from his firing position, his face a mask of blood.

The wounds being inflicted were terrible ones, because the men on the outside had no cover. They simply knelt or lay in a line along the rock, and when they were hit, the fat .44 slugs tore through the length of their bodies until they were stopped by a bone or emerged, leaving gaping holes.

Already the line had been reduced by a half, and the remaining three marksmen were beginning to wriggle backwards towards the sentinel rock. Luckily, he had chosen to watch from the west side of the slab while the faint trail swung around to the east.

The gun battle came to an end when two horsemen emerged from the dust cloud at the same time, firing together. One of them had a shotgun, and the buckshot scoured the shelf where the ambushers had waited, wounding one of the surviving three. It was a bloody, ugly wound, and the man screamed agonizingly.

His colleagues made no attempt to

help him, but simply turned tail and ran. The two horsemen fired after them, without scoring another hit. One of them rode over to the screaming man and looked down at him.

'Shut up!' he said. To Horn's amazement, the screaming gave way to agonizing moaning. The horsemen, shotgun in hand, leaned out of his saddle to examine the wound, but made no attempt to dismount or help.

'Help me,' begged the wounded man. The horseman laughed.

'You been rebranding our cattle for days, you ambush us because we found your hideout and you want me to help you? Help yourself. You been helping yourself to our beeves for long enough.'

He was turning away when the wounded man scrabbled for his handgun. His wounded shoulder would not do what he wanted, and the gun rattled across the rock. The horseman turned back.

'Back-shooter!' he said and let go with both barrels of the shotgun. Even to Horn, who had seen more battle-fields than he cared to remember, the act was one of true brutality. The wounded man's head and shoulders simply disappeared in a red mist.

The second horseman had ridden to the entrance to the canyon and seen the remaining two ambushers riding away. Now he returned, dismounted, and was examining the other bodies and emptying their pockets.

'Anything?' said the shotgun man. The searcher shook his head.

'The usual,' he said. 'This one's got a wanted poster on him. Ain't a good likeness, though. No wonder they never caught him. And there's some cash.'

'Ain't you going to split it with me?' said Shotgun. There was that in his voice which would have made Horn move carefully in the same situation, but the looter was counting the cash and was distracted.

'Not much,' he said. 'Couple of gold pieces on this one, but the rest's small change.'

'We'll split it,' said Shotgun. 'I'll take the gold. You can have the change.'

At last, his tone of voice registered with the dismounted man. He was caught with both hands full and his rifle lying by his feet. When he looked up, he was looking into the barrels of the shotgun, and Horn knew from experience what that looked like: a railroad tunnel with death coming down it, fast.

'Now, be reasonable,' the man said desperately. 'You can have the gold. I don't want it. We done what we come up here to do. We got rid of them rustlers, we found their hideout. We even found Injun Jim. We went up five and we come back two. No need for any more killing.'

'But there is,' said Shotgun, and pulled the trigger. The charge nearly cut the dismounted man in two.

Shotgun dismounted, picked the gold pieces out of the wreckage of his former colleague's hands, and wiped them on the remains of the dead man's shirt.

Then he did his best to pat himself

clean, though with the usual lack of success, and stood for a moment, looking round the carnage the canyon had turned into.

'To the winner, the spoils,' he said to himself, then laughed as though he had said something genuinely funny, and dropped the shotgun into the saddle boot. As he reached for the saddle horn to remount, Horn stepped out from behind the sentinel rock, and walked into the middle of the trail.

The gunman was busy gathering up the horses of his dead colleagues, and did not notice Horn until he turned towards the entrance. He stopped, and the horses bunched behind him.

'Who the hell might you be?'

Horn's Henry was in the crook of his right arm and his left hand was hooked into his belt, obscuring the butt of his second Colt. He looked more like a man going hunting than anything else. But then, he thought, that was exactly what he was.

'Well, now. I might be the Bull o'

Bashan,' he said easily. 'Then again, I might be the ghost of George Washington. But I ain't. I'm the man who's been stealing your cattle and rebranding them.'

The expressions which crossed Shotgun's face were worth seeing. First fury, then comprehension, and now a cunning immobility which spoke louder than an election speech. His eye flickered a look at the shotgun butt near his hand, and then away again.

He was wearing a military holster with a flap and Horn could see that the flap was buttoned down. Shotgun's eyes flickered towards the shotgun again, and then at the Henry still tucked harmlessly under Horn's right arm.

Horn watched him working it out. Maybe, if he was quick, he could get the shotgun into action before Horn could bring the Henry from under his arm.

What he needed was a diversion. Horn watched him working it out, and smiled, gently.

'Want to get down? I need a horse, and yours probably looks all right under all that dust. I reckon I'll have yours. And the others, of course. We'll need a good remuda when we put the ranch back together. You've brought us some fine beef to get started with.'

'That ain't yours!' He was talking to gain time and divert Horn's attention, and his hand was stealing towards the shotgun butt. He leaned forward over the saddle horn to mask the movement.

Horn saw the determination to try for the shotgun come into the man's eyes. He almost felt ashamed of himself, but he could smell the blood from the corpses all round him, and he thought it was time to call a halt on Shotgun.

The hand went out and grabbed the shotgun, the gunman bent forward over his horse's neck, he levelled the weapon. There were two sharp clicks.

'I was going to tell you,' Horn said conversationally. 'You forgot to reload after you murdered your friend. Fatal mistake, is that.'

He pulled the Colt from his belt and shot the rustler cleanly between the hating eyes.

Then he tumbled the body from the horse and, holding the reins, took the two gold pieces from the dead man's pockets. After a moment's thought he searched until he found some shotgun cartridges as well, reloaded the shotgun, and slipped it into the boot.

He rode down from the canyon of death leading a string of horses, and packing a small arsenal of small arms and ammunition.

Rules of war, he told himself. To the victor belong the spoils.

There remained the biggest villain of them all.

Morgan Fetterman, the man who had seeded all the evil in this valley, still had to be weeded out. It would, he thought, make the world a cleaner place. The world deserved it.

15

The girl and Sauermann were waiting out on the valley floor when he came from behind the rock. They had a small fire going and a coffee pot bubbling, and he could smell the coffee a hundred yards away.

He rode up to them, and fixed Sauermann with a stare as sharp as a stiletto.

'Don't blame me,' said the old man, nervously. 'She wouldn't go any further. Said she'd be too far away to help out when you needed it. Made me brew coffee in case you was hurt.'

Horn glanced at the girl who was bending over the fire, pouring coffee. She met his look with a stare of limpid innocence, and handed him a mug of coffee. It was strong as a buffalo bull and very sweet.

'How did you know,' he asked.

'I know you better than you realize,' she said.

'How come?'

'I studied the subject. I'm a good study.'

Their eyes met and he realized he was looking into the future. Somehow, it didn't look too bad.

'What are we going to do, now?' asked Sauermann. He sounded embarrassed.

'Why, we're going to clear the vermin out of the ranch house and clean it ready for human occupation,' she said. 'Aren't we, Luke Horn?'

'That we are, Miz Penrose. That we are.'

★   ★   ★

They put their newly acquired horses in a temporary corral to the north of the ranch house, rode down to the patch of woodland where he and Sauermann had hidden theirs on the night they rescued Jemima, and went to the edge of the trees to survey the ranch in the twilight.

There were no cattle there now. Where the meadows near the water had been filled with stolen beef there was only trodden ground. The water pump driven by a rickety windmill still squeaked rhythmically in the failing light. It was a scene which should have been peaceful, but somehow was filled with menace.

'Where'd they go?' Jemima asked after a short wait. 'There were two outfits based on the ranch house. That means at least ten saddle stock in the corrals near the house, and there isn't a single one. And where's the cattle? There was a whole herd down near the water. We slipped some of the rebrands into it.'

Sauermann was getting uneasy, and it showed.

'It's very quiet,' he said eventually.

'If you say 'too quiet' I'll slap you,' she said. 'Last time I was in Prescott they had a theatrical company in, doing

The Murder in the Blue Barn, and they said it every third line.'

Horn slid back away from the fringe of the woods and stood up. If the ranch house was in fact empty it would not do any harm to wait for daylight to make sure. If it was a trap, there would be some movement by morning. In the meantime, he decided to scout the surroundings in the dark.

'Fed, you and Miz Penrose get a good hidy-hole and hunker down for the night. I'm going to take a look around, and then I'll come and find you.' He heard Jemima take a deep breath and knew she was about to argue the point.

'And if she don't do what she's told, tie her hand and foot,' he said. Sauermann gave an approving grunt, and Jemima hissed like a frustrated snake. He knew he would pay for that one, later, but he was ninety per cent sure the ranch house was a trap, and he did not want her wandering into it.

He became even more sure when he

slid, silent as a bear with its boots off, close to the pile of rocks which hid the entrance to the escape tunnel. All was silent, and nothing stirred.

But something should. It was full dark now and before moonrise, and the creatures of the night should be out and about their business. But still nothing stirred.

Undecided, he lay quiet where he was for a while. After a few minutes the night air brought him a scent which confirmed his suspicions. It was the smell of tobacco smoke, on the lightest of night airs. Fresh tobacco smoke. Someone was indulging himself in the middle of a night watch.

Where there was one, there would be others. If they were watching the outside end of the escape tunnel, there would be others at the inside end. He needed to get out of there, and fast.

But as he started to move backwards, he heard a suppressed cough behind him. He rolled on his back. Nothing happened.

He began to move again, and had travelled only a few yards when he smelled the tobacco smoke again, more strongly this time. There was the faintest suggestion of a warm glow off to his left which meant that he had somehow come through the line of watchers and was now between them and the entrance to the tunnel.

He lay silent for a while, listening for movement and managed to identify three. There was the smoker; behind him was a man with an irritating cough which he kept trying to suppress, off to the left; and a scratcher who had at least one flea in his clothes to the right. He was surrounded.

When detection is inevitable, he decided, lie back and enjoy.

'Who the hell is smoking?' he hissed in a whisper which could have been heard in Tucson. There was a startled movement off to his right and a muffled cough. He suspected the smoker had just inhaled his cigarette and suppressed an insane desire to giggle.

'I said, 'Who the hell is smoking' and I want to hear an answer,' he all but bellowed.

'Ain't me, boss,' came from his left and worryingly close behind him. Another denial came from the right.

'So it's you, is it? Answer me!'

The third denial was wheezed. There was no fourth, and he stood up making no attempt to disguise his movements.

'Don't think I'll forget this,' he hissed. 'I'll be back, and there better be no smoke around, then. They could be here now for all you know.'

He walked away, making no attempt to move quietly, and put as much distance between himself and the tunnel as he could before swinging to make for the grove of trees where they had left the horses.

Since their horses had been found there before, he approached the spot carefully, but there was no waiting ambush here.

Trouble was, there were no horses, either.

He stood in the cover of a juniper trunk, and examined the moonlit scene. He could see where they had tethered the horses, in a stand of junipers, but they were definitely not there any more.

He backed off and was working his way round to a better view of the site when a sharp hiss from the darkness stopped him in his tracks.

'Horn!' said a nearby cypress in Sauermann's voice. 'Come this way and walk soft. There's a couple of rustlers over towards the house.'

He walked soft until a hand caught at his sleeve and pulled him down into the cover of a tree. The cypress grew thick down near the ground and made good cover.

'They ain't got our horses,' Sauermann murmured in his ear. 'Miz Penrose got 'em back there a ways, with that darned shotgun in her hands. We better be careful when we get back or we're like to get cut in half. This way.'

He was off like a coyote, swift and silent, and close to the ground. Horn followed as best he could, but the journey was not a long one.

'They got the house surrounded, but they ain't all that many of them,' Sauermann reported when they were out of earshot of the watchers in the woods. 'We reckon maybe ten at most, two here, two in the stable with the horses, there's at least one man in the house, and if they're running to form, they'll have another two on the other side.'

'Plus three watching the passageway,' said Horn. 'You're right, that makes ten. Three each. Plus one.'

Sauermann shook his head in the moonlight. 'I found one of the men in the woods by himself. He ain't coming back,' he said.

Nine, then. It would be a good idea to take out another one at his sentry post, silently. Silent deaths in the dark would make the already jumpy rustlers spooked almost beyond bearing. Nervous men were liable to shoot one another in the dark as easily as their enemies.

'Think we can take another one?'

The old man grinned, a ghastly sight in the moonlight.

'I got just the candidate,' he said. 'Want it noisy or silent? Noisy? Wait here.'

The scream, when it came, was blood-curdling, a shriek of pain which rose in the moonlight as though from another world, and trailed off with a sob. Nervous men already keyed up to fever pitch simply could not help themselves. They fired at every moving shadow they saw until somebody shouted them into silence.

But the ambush was already broken. One after another, the watchers in the woods gave up and made their way back to the ranch house. Two horses were saddled and ridden away into the darkness.

'That leaves six, assuming there's only one in the house,' said Jemima, sitting with her back against one stone and her feet against another. 'When do we take the ranch back?'

Sauermann shook his head. 'Don't be so all-fired eager to get yourself killed, girl — I mean, ma'am. We lucked out so far because they don't know we're here. Far as we know, they still think it's other owlhoots sneaking up behind them.'

'But them bad actors is hard and nasty. Soon's they find out there ain't but three of us, a young girl, a grandpappy and a gunfighter with the crippled arm, they'll get their bravery back so fast it'll make your head spin. And they'll find that out as soon as we come out of the woodwork.'

They were within sight of the ranch house when the dawn came, behind a shallow fold in the ground which hid the horses, using Horn's field glasses in turn to keep an eye on the place. Smoke came from the kitchen chimney, but apart from that there was no sign of life.

'Hey, looky here,' said Sauermann suddenly when it was his turn to watch. Horn and Jemima, who had been avoiding one another's eyes, hunkered down next to him. But he was not looking at the ranch house, but down the trail which led to the eastern entrance to the valley.

They could see the rider coming along at a stately pace, and even without the glasses Horn could see the horse was a fine animal.

'Fetterman?' he said.

'Fetterman,' confirmed Jemima, who had snatched the glasses against Sauermann's protests. 'Looks like he's dressed for a Sunday meeting, too. He isn't going to like what he finds here. Not after he set out so fine and early.'

She was right. Fetterman's magnificent self-possession and poise took quite a kicking when he heard the tale of the night's events. He appeared on the ranch house porch with the rustlers around him, and to judge from his arm gestures and their resentful stares he was raving like a madman.

Eventually, one of the rustlers decided he had enough. He walked away to the barn, and reappeared a few minutes later, leading his horse. The others watched while he mounted the animal and turned him away towards the valley entrance.

It was too much for Fetterman. He ran to his horse, and pulled the fine custom-built rifle from the saddle boot. He turned to aim it at the departing horseman. The man glanced over his shoulder, saw what was happening, and threw himself down over his horse's neck, kicking in the spurs.

The act saved his life, for the first shot raised a spurt of dirt directly in line with where he had been. Fetterman worked the lever and had another try and then another. The racing horseman, jinking as though he was roping steers, at last got too far away for accurate shooting, and the impotent Fetterman turned back to the ranch house only to find two of the riders were there.

He was in time to see that the rest of the depleted band were in the process of saddling their horses. One of them

214

was watching Fetterman and holding a Winchester poised to shoot. The former criminal king wisely dropped his rifle and watched them saddle up and mount.

The last act from one of them was to ride over and pick up the custom-made rifle. He examined it briefly, and then laid it across his knees as he turned away. The rifle went with him.

Fetterman watched as they rode away from him, the end of a grandiose dream of a criminal empire such as Arizona had never seen, as he liked to call it.

'Kinda sad, ain't it?' said a voice behind him.

He spun on his heel to find himself looking at the true owner of the valley, flanked by her old ranch hand and the man Fetterman had hired to kill her.

They were looking at him as though he had two heads, both of them ugly.

'How the hell . . . ?' he said. He stopped because Horn put his finger to his lips and shook his head.

'There's a lady present,' he said. 'Use

bad language in front of her again, and I'm gonna take offence. You won't like me when I take offence, Fetterman.'

He swung down from his horse, for one second turning his shoulder to Fetterman and the man noticed that his right arm hung loose by his side.

A crippled gunfighter? That was worth knowing. He could feel his own left elbow against the hideaway Colt he carried under his coat. It was a short-barrelled model with the trigger guard cut away, and the shells had been cut across the nose to make a deep cross. When they struck their target, they expanded to leave a terrible wound. Few men survived what would normally be a flesh wound.

But the girl had a rifle across her knees and the old cowpoke looked, on closer inspection, to be made of bile and rawhide.

Well, he had been in worse fixes and shot his way out. If he shot the girl first — a pity, but sacrifices had to be made — he could get the old man, who did

216

not have his pistol drawn. The crippled gunfighter would not believe the speed at which Fetterman could kill, and since his injury was on his right side, it was bound to slow him down.

The man was down from his horse, but his right side was still turned away, which would slow him down more. The girl and the old man started to dismount. It was his moment.

'Say goodbye to your whore!' he said, and the specialized Colt dropped into his hand as he turned towards her.

But she was not there. For a moment, he was confused, then he saw her legs below the horse's belly. He could not hit her, but he could take out the men.

He switched targets smoothly and his finger felt the trigger as his thumb drew back the hammer. He heard the gunshots, wondered where they were coming from. Tried to fire back.

But the weapon simply fired into the ground by his own feet. Puzzled, he tried to draw back the hammer again, but the weapon fell from his hand as though he had lost all strength. He tried to raise his eyes to look at Horn, and the effort was monumental. With one last effort he managed a slight movement. He heard his own voice saying: 'But how?'

'Because you're a dead man,' Horn told him. But he was talking to a corpse.

Afterword

They sat on the porch drinking coffee and watched the boys and their sister breaking horses in the home corral. It was a lively process and they both tensed when one bronco bucked and sunfished at the same time, throwing its rider in a graceful arc before hitting the ground.

But the outriders closed in on the horse, and kept it away while the rider clambered back to her feet.

'Might have known she'd bounce,' said Horn as he relaxed. His wife glanced at him and grinned.

'Tessa's as good a rider as any of the boys. Why don't you admit it?' she teased. Her husband glanced at her under his eyebrows.

'She's better except for Fed,' he said. 'That boy can stay on anything alive including a grizzly bear and a wildcat.'

His wife laughed delightedly.

'But then, who'd dare to get off one of them!' they chorused and burst into a roar of laughter. Down at the corral, their sons and daughter looked at one another and grinned.

'But then, who'd *want* to get off one of them?' they chorused. 'Once you got off, they'd eat you!'

We do hope that you have enjoyed reading this large print book.

Did you know that all of our titles are available for purchase?

We publish a wide range of high quality large print books including:
Romances, Mysteries, Classics
General Fiction
Non Fiction and Westerns

Special interest titles available in large print are:
The Little Oxford Dictionary
Music Book, Song Book
Hymn Book, Service Book

Also available from us courtesy of Oxford University Press:
Young Readers' Dictionary
(large print edition)
Young Readers' Thesaurus
(large print edition)

For further information or a free brochure, please contact us at:
Ulverscroft Large Print Books Ltd.,
The Green, Bradgate Road, Anstey,
Leicester, LE7 7FU, England.
Tel: (00 44) **0116 236 4325**
Fax: (00 44) **0116 234 0205**

DAUGHTER OF EVIL

H. H. Cody

When Jake Probyn hauls up outside the Circle F ranch, he's looking for work, not trouble. But he finds trouble in the shape of the boss's daughters and the foreman, Ransome. Things get worse when the old man dies leaving the ranch to his daughters. Then there are back shootings, range fires and one daughter goes missing . . . and while the Drowned Valley on Circle F land has its own eerie story to tell, there's trouble galore waiting for Jake . . .